HOLOGRAM:
A HAUNTING

09-17-2019

HOLOGRAM:
A HAUNTING

To Chris
and Ed —

Enjoy
the chills —

AUTHOR OF THE POLAND TRILOGY
JAMES CONROYD MARTIN

James Conroyd Martin

HUSSAR
QUILL PRESS

CHICAGO

For Scott H. Hagensee

ALSO BY
JAMES CONROYD MARTIN

THE POLAND TRILOGY
Push Not the River Book One
Against a Crimson Sky Book Two
The Warsaw Conspiracy Book Three

ACKNOWLEDGMENTS

THIS NOVEL WOULD NOT HAVE been possible without the inspiration of Scott Hagensee, his research into the history of a particular Hammond house, the family that had it built, and the characteristics of Hammond, Indiana, in 1910-11. Moreover, occurrences experienced in the house provided the impetus of the fictional story.

Kudos go to editor extraordinaire Mary Rita Perkins Mitchell for her editing skills and incisive continuity suggestions.

This is one of those books writers sometimes set aside for a while. It was brought to the forefront first by Kathryn Mitchell and then by John Rdzak, Ellen Longawa, Linda Hansen, and by master of the science fiction and fantasy genres, Piers Anthony.

Angels, and ministers of grace, defend us!
Be thou a spirit of health, or goblin damn'd.
Bring with thee airs from heaven, or blasts from hell.
Be thy intents wicked or charitable.
Thou com'st in such a questionable shape …

Shakespeare, Hamlet 1.4

PROLOGUE

HAMMOND, INDIANA
JULY 1911

"D AMN!" NINE-YEAR-OLD CLAUDE REICHART WHISPERED under his breath as he kicked a stone across the gravel drive that led to the old barn. His father's favorite curse tasted good on his tongue. Good enough to repeat it, louder. He kicked again. The dust of a dry summer lifted, eddied, and slowly settled, its effect pleasing the boy.

He looked up at the barn that was being used as a garage, squinting in the glare of the sun. His wire-rimmed spectacles had become dusty. He removed them and wiped the lenses with a hanky, all the while mesmerized by the fading and blistering red of the barn.

Forbidden territory.

Claude replaced the spectacles and looked sideways, to the house. He knew he should return to the swing on the verandah. But it would be another hour, his mother had told him, before he would play for the church ladies, who would whisper and coo and nod, fans flashing and huge hats bobbing. He deemed most of them silly women, their doting something to endure. He was anxious to be back at the black and white keys, feeling the vibration and noise and power of the music at his command. It was only then that he felt happy.

Now, for once he wished he had a friend to help ease his boredom. Not that he got any pleasure out of the kind of play children his own age found fun.

Claude was too smart not to be aware of his difference from other children. He did have a vague recollection of that day, at four years old, when his father sat him down on a stool in front of a new upright Steinway. Or perhaps his father had repeated the story so many times that he merely thought he remembered. But he could not recall a time before the piano. Music, it seemed had been his existence always, as much a part of him as breathing. His father often remarked that playing and inventing melodies came to him as if to a bird. Mr. Schmidt, the music master his father had hired, agreed.

The heat of the noon sun stung Claude's face and arms and legs, and the discomfort prompted Claude to move. Ahead of him, temptation beckoned. He started slowly toward the two-story structure that housed the family's two electric cars.

He knew the barn was full of curiosities from the past. Harnesses, riding crops, and implements from the days when the land had been farm land. Things to examine, wonder at, touch. Things more modern, too, like the mysteriously massive and intricate transformers that charged the family cars. There was danger in electricity, his father had warned, but Claude was thinking now that it would be cool inside.

After ten or twelve paces, he brought himself up short. He paused, listening to the lilting cadences of the women's laughter, his mother's soprano ringing above the others'.

He sucked in a long breath. He knew that he should return to the verandah, that his mother would look for him there. And yet . . .

He removed his spectacles and wiped at them again. By the time he put them back on, his indecision had evaporated.

His body lurched into motion, and with just a few quick and furtive steps, he slipped into the structure his father had proclaimed *verboten*.

———————⚬•⚭•⚬———————

"Where is the child?" Polly Davis questioned. "When shall we hear him play?"

Alicia Reichart nodded in the direction of the dining room door that led out onto the verandah. "Claude's out on the swing. He'll play for us after luncheon."

"Oh, we are so looking forward to it," Polly said in her throaty voice, nodding to her cluster of friends as if she spoke for all. "You are so fortunate, my dear, having a child like that. A prodigy, the paper says."

"Everyone says that!" Mabel Tryon said.

Alicia Reichart smiled. She *was* lucky, she knew. Life had certainly blessed her and she thanked God every day for her poor but happy childhood, a fine husband, wealth, status in her church and community—and most of all, little Claude. The tow-headed, green-eyed child was the joy of her days. He was her future. His name—Claude Reichart—would one day be revered along with the masters like Liszt, Chopin, Mozart. And she would be right there with him on his journey toward immortality. She shivered. How *had* she become so fortunate?

Although Hammond had been a thriving Midwest city since the turn of the century and now boasted a bustling downtown center and three opera houses, it would be the name of Reichart that would put it on the map there at the bottom of Lake Michigan in letters large enough to elicit notice, real notice. Alicia had her worries, however. She knew that her son's talent was destined to one day take him from Hammond. Would it take him from her, as well? There already had been overtures from abroad. Her husband Jason had spent a year in Paris after law school and favored a school there. Would she be able to send Claude away? Or, if she were to go along, could she part with her husband and the two-year-old twin boys? That Jason could go was out of the question. The family law firm held its considerable success to his involvement on every level.

"Is the stained glass from the Tiffany Company?" The question pulled Alicia from her thoughts. It came from Ruth Mason, a newcomer to the First Presbyterian Church and so a new guest at 33 Springfield Street.

"Yes," Alicia Reichart replied, holding in check her pride. She dared not appear smug. That is another thing, she thought. This house! How am I ever to leave this house?

They sat in the music room and the conversation turned to other things. Alicia's eyes were focused on the horizontal panel of three square windows above the Steinway. The sunshine caught every flashing nuance of the glass, both clear and frosted, and of the hues of green and amber. The side windows opened inward and were adjusted now only so far as to admit fresh air, while still allowing for the pleasure of the eye. All three were to have been stationary, like the massive triptych vertical panels on the staircase, but she had insisted that the two side windows be made to open. Although the room had two ordinary windows on the west wall, she knew the western sun could be brutal and that when the shades on those windows had to be drawn, the family would relish a breeze from the north. Jason had seen to it that she confer with the architect on such things throughout the planning and building stages.

Such activities naturally took her away from her children and for this she had felt some sense of guilt. But they did not want for good care and—oddly—it seemed as if the new home had become for her another child.

Nearly a mile due south of the city's center, the house was the first on a street newly developed on the old Hayley farmstead. The architect had blended the most beautiful and functional aspects of the Greek, Federal, and other styles. Facing south, away from the sprawling city, the sixteen-room house of planking with its Doric columns and wide windows sat perched like a large unblinking matron in starched white. The views east and south from the balconies were of Indiana's breathtakingly lush green farmland and prairie studded with purple and yellow flowers. Just a stone's throw to the west, across the state line into Illinois, lay the rustic village of West Hammond. Behind and a bit east of the great square structure, at the end of a gravel drive, sat the old Hayley barn. It was an eyesore and Alicia looked forward to the fall when a proper coach house would be erected for their electric carriages, white as the house and replete with living quarters above for a servant or two.

⸺◦❦◦⸺

Upon the sound of his mother's voice, Claude Reichart peered down from the hayloft window. His mother stood on the back porch speaking sharply to Della, the kitchen maid. His mother's face looked mean, a meanness mirrored by Butch and Sally, the family dogs who had trailed her. She was scolding the Irish maid for taking time away from her luncheon duties to bring a plate of food out to a hobo. Claude was used to seeing such men, who came through Hammond on freight trains, sometimes stopping in town long enough to find their way south to Springfield Street and the big white house. Drifters, Papa called them. He often warned Claude to steer clear of them. Some could be very dangerous, he said in his deep, disapproving way.

The old hobo was large, his face red beneath a tangled mass of greasy hair, dark but graying. Claude felt the man's embarrassment. Or is it anger? he wondered. Papa's face would turn just as red on those few occasions when he became very angry.

Claude's mother hustled the maid into the house and in the exchange the contents of the plate—chicken salad, beans, corn bread—fell to the ground. The German Shepherds tore into it at once. His mother's face softened a bit, and she told the man to come back later in the day if he wished food.

After she had gone in, the man attempted to salvage some of the food, but the dogs' low growls were menacing enough to dissuade him. They were not about to share. Incensed, he kicked at the dirt and moved away, out of Claude's sightline.

Claude turned from the window and started to move toward the opening leading down. He knew that he should get back to the verandah. After that little scene he had just witnessed, his mother would be completely out of sorts if she were to find him gone. She insisted that her luncheons go off like clockwork, and could be quite a bear to live with—so his father said—when they didn't. Besides, it would not be long before he would be called in to play. And he had a new piece he was anxious to try out.

His hands had only just touched the ladder that jutted up into the loft when he heard a noise from below. He stopped, his heart pausing as well, then racing.

Wide sliding doors were situated at both the front and back of the barn. It was one of the doors at the rear that was creaking slowly open now, strangely so. A widening angle of light poured in—and with it the gigantic shadow of the hobo in the doorway. He had merely made the pretense of leaving the property, disappearing instead around the rear of the barn and out of sight of the house.

Damn. What am I to do now? Claude was not supposed to be in the barn, much less in the hayloft. Only last week he had begged permission. His father's words rang in his ears now: *What if you were to fall and break an arm or hand? You might never play the same way again!*

The boy trembled. His grip on the ladder tightened. How was he to avoid this man, this hungry and angry man who had lost his chance at a good meal?

Of what terrible things was such a man capable? He had been warned about the transients who came and went with the trains.

Claude stared down. The light that had filled the downstairs suddenly disappeared. The door had been shut again.

He listened.

The man was inside the barn. Claude's heart hammered in his chest. He could hear the man shuffling about below in the shadows, mumbling unhappily to himself.

Then the man came into view, the top of his head framed— as if by a camera—in the square opening leading downstairs. Claude held his breath, praying the man did not look up. Slowly, noiselessly, the boy drew away from the ladder. His head reeled. He sensed danger. He was not usually afraid of strangers, but he felt something stir inside him, something as instinctive as his talent. Something poisonous.

He would not try to get past the man. He would wait.

He swallowed hard, his stomach turning. *Why have I done this? I've been warned.*

Claude heard a familiar metallic noise now. He inched his way to where he could peer down again. He knelt on the floor and brought his head low until he could make out what the intruder was doing. His father had taken his own car to the law office, so it was his mother's Woods Victoria that had caught the man's interest. He was leaning inside now, as if fishing for something.

Claude drew back, wondering if he should attempt the ladder . . . if he were quick enough . . . But when he looked again the man was sitting on the hard ground, absorbed in a paper package he had found. A match flared in the gloom. The man had found Claude's father's cigarettes—or did they belong to his mother?

The rising sulfur and cigarette smoke caused Claude to move back, slowly, carefully. The smell had always caused him to sneeze. He felt a sneeze welling up now and held his breath.

He prayed for the urge to pass. He prayed very hard.

The man won't stay, Claude told himself. He'll be too afraid of getting caught.

The inclination to sneeze passed.

The boy lay down soundlessly on a soft mound of old hay, curling into a fetal position, praying that the man would not venture up the ladder. I'll just wait him out, he thought. He's bound to go soon.

Time passed.

———◦◦◦———

Claude was right. The strange man did rise to leave soon after he finished several cigarettes, but he had stayed long enough for the sense of danger to slow, like Claude's pulse, coaxing the boy into slumber.

One arm was not enough for the man to pull open the wide carriage door. He grunted to himself and freed the other by tossing aside the butt of his last cigarette.

———◦◦◦———

Although the chicken salad hadn't been seasoned in the way she liked—too much pepper, too little poultry seasoning—Alicia Reichart smiled to herself at the way the luncheon was progressing. She prayed that the nanny would be able to keep the twin boys contained once they were awakened from their naps and the recital began.

Overseeing two men hired for the occasion, she was trying to fit as many chairs into the modest music room as she could manage. Only twenty could be accommodated. Some guests would have to be seated in the hall and double parlor. Perhaps, she thought, next time it would be better to have the piano moved to the dining room so that more people could appreciate the sight as well as the sound of little Claude's playing.

"Alicia!" Julia Mulvihill's shrill cry wrenched Alicia from her thoughts. "Alicia! Come at once, there's a fire!"

A cry of alarm rose among the ladies, who were all on their feet in a great crush, pushing toward the dining room door that led outside. They spilled out onto the columned verandah that flanked the driveway, their faces—like a stage of tragic masks—drawn to the north, their cries rising at what met their eyes.

Alicia pushed through a mass of trailing dresses, silk and laces, shoulders and elbows. Her heart thumped wildly.

What was afire? Was it a fire downtown? The Lion Store? Her mind would not work.

Then she saw the smoke coming up onto the verandah and realized how close the fire must be.

When she got to the door, she could feel the fire's heat and did not look to the left—in the direction of the barn—for she had already determined what it was that was ablaze. Those bulky transformers had given her shivers of fear the very day they were installed. She knew it was the barn and so she shouldered her way onto the porch, looking instead to the right, to the porch swing where she prayed to find Claude sitting.

The swing was empty, completely still.

Her frantic eyes swept the crowded porch for her son. Her heart caught.

"Sweet Jesus in Heaven!" The shrill oath came from Polly Davis. Similar piercing cries and screams rose from the other women. Something terrible had claimed their attention.

Clara Douglas fainted.

Martha Grimes tried to soldier Alicia into the house. Alicia fended her off. She would not be moved.

Pulling free, she turned to see the flames and smoke enveloping the old barn, rendering it a blazing inferno. She could hear the sounds of crackling, splintering wood.

And she saw now, for just a moment before the smoke thickened, what the others had seen. There at the cracked window of the hayloft loomed a blanched and bespectacled face. Claude's face. Behind the dirty glass, the twisted lips mouthed the unmistakable syllables: *Ma-ma. Ma-ma.*

Now, as if in a slow, surreal dream, tentacles of smoke enfolded him and the pale form fell back from sight.

ONE

CHICAGO, ILLINOIS
1999

MARGARET FLAHERTY ROCKWELL HAD TWO secrets. The first, that she had seen a ghost, she had—for the moment—forgotten.

It was her second secret that was her ally in this, the first real argument of her two-year marriage.

"Martini?" Kurt called from the little kitchen.

"No thanks," she heard herself say. She bit at her lower lip. *Yes*, she wanted to say, *with three olives*. Meg listened to the steel and glass tinkling sounds of the quiet, ordered ritual. He's so certain he'll have his way, she thought.

She stared out the window, her hands interlocked and unconsciously resting on her belly. The northeast view from the twenty-sixth floor was breathtaking: the park, the golf course, the tiny cars—like her nephew's hot wheels—following the curve of Lake Shore Drive, and the incomparable lakefront. The view was unobstructed because far below sat the historically designated Pattington, where one of her friends, Wenonah Smythe resided. It was a wonderful old sprawling complex of condominiums that had been—at the turn of the century—rather elite apartments. While out walking, she often found herself daring to breach the walkways in the double courtyards so that she could stare into the oversized windows, some of which held wondrously curved glass. So much more history in a building like that!

But it wasn't only the characterless feel of the thirty-year-old building they currently occupied that rankled. Or even the vertigo, with which she had wrestled since childhood. No, the fact that this was his condo she had moved into made her feel unsettled, ill-at-ease. Not hers. Not theirs. Oh, she had told herself that moving into Kurt's bachelor condo would be fine. And yet, somehow, it wasn't.

Meg wished that she could steel herself with a martini. But there would be no drinking for a while.

"Sure you don't want anything?" Kurt asked, coming out of the small area that he called a kitchen.

"No," Meg said. She thought of the house she had fallen in love with and took strength from the image. She would have it—or rather, they would.

Kurt sat next to her on the sofa. She didn't turn to watch him; she didn't have to. Her mind's eye pictured him sipping at the martini as if it were liquid confidence. The blond hair—not a strand of gray visible—fell forward as he bent over the glass, hiding for the moment those blue eyes that could so coolly charm. Too damned boyish-looking for thirty-nine, Meg thought. Did she look the younger by two years? Did she look younger at all? Even with the silver which had begun to invade her reddish brown hair?

Not that Meg was wanting in self-esteem. She never had been. She kept herself in shape although she worried sometimes about her classic Irish look. Someone had told her—who was it? Father?—that Celtic beauty faded faster in alien climates. Still, that hadn't kept her out of the sun as a teenager. She knew how well a little color brought out her green eyes. *Emeralds*, Kurt—with his Germanic lineage—called them. *Like the Isle itself* she would answer.

"Dee-licious," Kurt purred.

He's doing his corny schtick, Meg thought. She didn't respond.

"Not too late," he said. "You can have this one, and I'll make another."

"No, thanks." Meg drew in a deep breath. "Kurt, what I want is the house."

There, it was out!

"Oh, for Chrissakes, Meg!"

She sat silent, continuing to stare out, listening to the March winds whip around the building. The lake was dark and cold looking, free of vessels. She could feel his eyes on her.

Her silence was annoying him.

"We went to see it on a lark, didn't we?" Kurt asked, sipping at his drink. "Because that nurse in cardio-pulmonary said it was a real find. Like something out of the Old South and cheap. We went to look, Meg. It was a little day trip. We didn't go out there to *buy* a house, Meg—and in Indiana, for Chrissakes!"

"It's only thirty minutes away."

"From here?" Kurt scoffed. "When?—At three in the morning, maybe."

"I can get a job out there. You know I hate what's going on at the hospital. All the politics. And the days of the medical social worker are numbered."

"Great! And what about me? I've worked my ass off to get where I am. I'm a vice-president now, Meg. What about my fricking career?"

"I'm not suggesting you quit. You could commute."

"Do you know what the expressways are like at rush hour?"

"The South Shore train will take you right into downtown Hammond."

Kurt laughed. "Downtown Hammond—yeah, right!"

"You say that like it's an oxymoron."

"A what?"

"Never mind. Hammond is coming back, didn't the realtor say so? And those who invest now in the historic district— "

"Are going to be shit out of luck when they find their realtors are just trying to make a living. Like I do—in Chicago!" Kurt lifted the nearly empty glass as if to toast the lakeshore.

They sat in silence several minutes, watching dusk fall and listening to the whoosh of traffic on the drive and the occasional exclamation of a horn or siren.

Meg's gray-and-white cat, Rex, sidled up against her legs, then instead of jumping into her lap, he walked away as if he sensed the tension in the room. Meg watched as he carefully avoided the window ledge and the sharp drop that had terrified him the day they had moved into Kurt's condo. He had leaped onto the man-made marble windowsill, looked down, meowed in fright, and leaped to the safety of the sofa. The twenty-six stories above ground had not amused him. Truth was, the height had terrified them both.

How Rex will love the house, Meg thought.

Kurt spoke at last. "Meg, our friends and family are here in the city."

Ah, the tactful approach, Meg thought. "And the Cubs?" They were walking distance from Wrigley Field. "You see Sammy Sosa more often than you do your parents."

"Yeah, and the Cubs. Okay, I won't deny it. They plan even more night games now."

"I'm sure our Wrigleyville neighbors will be glad to hear that."

"Now, don't go cynical on me."

Meg turned to look at him now. "Kurt, it's not Alaska."

"It's a 1910 huge frame house, a money pit. Ever see that movie with Tom Hanks? Damned funny, but damned true. Meg, it's old and in disrepair. It's going to need everything—paint— "

"Roof, furnace, plumbing, and electric—we've been through all that. But at the price it's being offered we can do all that as needed."

He stared at her with what seemed amazement. "You really want this place, don't you?"

Meg nodded. "Yes."

Kurt sighed, and without taking his eyes off her, he set the empty martini glass on the steel and glass table she hated. "Why?"

"I—I don't quite know. I just want it." That Meg didn't know came as a sudden revelation to herself. She knew only that from the time she had seen it, it had, in some inexplicable way, become a part of her—or was it the other way around?

"It's a whim, then?" Kurt's question was more accusation.

"No, it's not!" Meg's immediate and strong reaction surprised even herself.

Kurt was staring at her in a way he never had before.

Had he seen through to her will in this matter? To a determination he had not expected? Was he weakening?

Meg was not about to be intimidated or bullied. Not now. Not about this. Her mother had told her to choose her fights, the ones worth fighting for.

He's going to concede now, she thought.

"Meg," he said, the blue eyes round as stones and as serious as she had ever seen, "I won't live in Hammond—no matter how beautiful, how historic, or how cheap the house is."

Meg's heart fell, rebounded. "It's a home, not a house."

"Okay, it's a home—but it's not ours, Meg."

His statement was meant to be the final word. He stood. "I think I'll have another drink. You're absolutely certain you don't want one?"

Meg shook her head. "Absolutely certain." The time had come to play her ace. "Kurt, you said we could one day relocate out of the city."

"Yeah, I guess I did. I said maybe if we start a family."

"No, you said *when* we start a family."

"Okay, when— "

"Kurt, when is now."

Kurt Rockwell retraced his steps and dropped down onto the sofa, his square jaw sagging. "You're not?" His eyes were widening into blue discs of surprise, happiness, childish reprimand.

Meg said nothing.

His gaze moved down, his expression registering the protective way Meg was holding her belly.

Meg smiled.

Kurt tried to speak but couldn't.

Instead, he reached out for her, pulled her to him, held her. It was not something he did often and the action came a beat or two behind spontaneity, but Meg responded, warmed by his touch. They kissed.

Kurt drew back, launching into a litany of questions: how long had she suspected, when had her test proven positive, how did she feel then, how does she feel now?

One by one, she addressed the questions, assuring him that she was delighted and feeling perfect.

"Now I really do need another drink!" Kurt announced, springing up. "Oh, my God!" he blurted, flushed with excitement and pride. There had been no children in his first marriage. "And I'll get you some mineral water, young lady!"

Meg lost no time in following up. *Strike while the iron is hot.* Her father had such a fondness for the adage. While Meg hated the cliché, she respected its core truth.

Before Kurt reached the kitchen, Meg made her own announcement. "Mrs. Shaw will be calling back at nine."

"Mrs. Shaw?"

"Yes, Kurt. The realtor."

———◦∘⊂⊘⊃∘◦———

Late into the night, Meg lay awake on her side, staring out to where a quarter moon shone on the darkly placid waters of Lake Michigan.

She had not played fair. She had used her pregnancy to get what she wanted. And after they had given the realtor a go-ahead to prepare a bid on the house, she had encouraged Kurt to make love to her. He had never been so gentle, and instead of easing her guilt at manipulating him, the lovemaking increased it.

But the guilt dissipated as she began to consider the child. The baby was what was important. I have life inside me, she thought, cradling her belly. As her single years had ticked by, she wondered whether this time would ever come. She could remember herself at thirteen telling her mother she would have seventeen children. The memory made her smile. She would settle for one now. This child would be her reason for living, sustaining her, renewing her. After all, her career in medical social work had not lived up to her expectations.

And her marriage . . .

Meg turned away from the window, switching to her other side and toward Kurt, who was sleeping soundly. She watched him. She was glad that he was pleased by the news. Perhaps the decision to marry him had been a good one. She had been doubtful. When his pursuit of her started, she had had her own pursuit: to have a child before time made it dangerous or impossible to do so. The problems facing a single mother didn't faze her, and she had spent the two years before dating Kurt exploring the several avenues that could lead her to motherhood, including adoption. She was determined to have a child.

The appearance of Kurt Rockwell in her life had been a Godsend, or so her mother said, and Meg thought perhaps she was right. He had loved her from the start, she was certain, in a straightforward—if less than impassioned—way of his own. He had been tireless in his attention, quietly persistent despite her initial rebuffs. She had told herself—when she finally agreed to marry him—that she would come to love him.

She took stock of her feelings now. Although she had come to care for him and worry with and about him in a day-to-day life of big concerns and little details, she knew that she didn't *love* Kurt.

At least not like she had loved Pete. Meg lay on her back now. Just the name conjured up those high school years. Golden years. Golden Peter Stoltmeyer. Two decades later her heart still raced at the thought of him.

Meg's family had just moved from Chicago to a suburb, Oak Park, and without friends her freshman year at Oak Park-River Forest High School had been a disaster. She went through it blindly, head down against the wind, looking forward only to graduation. But in sophomore year she met Pete. He came up to her locker one day and introduced himself.

High school came alive for Meg Flaherty at that moment. A whirling, blinding flash of friends, parties, fun, romance—but, most of all—Pete. Gregarious singer, basketball player, record-setting swimmer, inveterate poker player, passionate lover. The relationship developed, deepening until senior year when they made love for the first time in Pete's old pink Buick Electra convertible, the rain pouring down on the canvas-like roof and beading on the windows.

Pete was the only one from school that year accepted into Yale, but he vowed to decline the offer and go to the University of Iowa—with Meg. She had said nothing to bring him to that decision. He had come to it on his own—and she loved him for it, looking forward to their days in Iowa City.

In retrospect, she sensed something different about Pete in the weeks after graduation, but she had not seen the end moving toward her, like some terrible storm whipped up out of a perfect summer day. In July he told her he had changed his mind—at his parents' urging—and he was to go to Yale after all.

Sick inside, Meg took it with a smile. Despite what he said, what they said to each other, it was the end and she somehow sensed it. There were letters at first when the fall term started, but after Pete stayed out east for the semester break—his parents went to see him—communication fell off, and by the end of the second semester, stopped altogether. Had she stopped writing, certain that he would awaken to the void in his heart, certain that he would pick up the pursuit? The scenario that he would do so had been a fantasy of hers. Or had he stopped writing, his interests placed elsewhere?

What if distance hadn't separated them? she wondered.

Meg's eye traced a crack in the ceiling. Time is a strange thing, she thought. Twenty years and yet the passion and hurt remained so real, so fresh, like the death of an immediate family member. She could bring it to the surface in a heartbeat. She recalled a Bee Gees' song of the era about mending broken hearts, silly and maudlin to her adult mind, but it had been her anthem after Pete. Her heart hadn't mended; it had tired.

Meg was not one of those who could look back on her past and say, *Oh, it was just one of those high school romances. You know how it was.*

Meg did know how it was, couldn't forget, couldn't let time reduce it in perspective, and for years her memory was her worst enemy, still could be.

Kurt started to snore. He did that when he had had a few drinks. She turned her head to watch him, praying she had done the right thing in marrying him.

The child would make it right, she thought. *The child will make everything right.*

Meg thought back to the evening's argument and the question Kurt had asked, a simple question that somehow unnerved her: Why did she want the house so badly? In truth, she couldn't say. The white house on a triple lot—with its columns, balconies, mullioned windows, stained and leaded glass—was a steal, no doubt about it. But there was something more—a feeling or emotional connection much stronger than wood and glass at a bargain price—that had engaged her heart, some unnamable attraction or affinity to the place.

What was it?

And there was something else. On the day they had seen the house, Meg had witnessed a strange occurrence. Set back from and to the right of the house was a coach house, gray and dilapidated, its shutters askew. Kurt and Meg wondered if it was included in the low price. The realtor assured them that it was.

They had met Mrs. Shaw on the side of the house, halfway up the long gravel drive that led to the coach house. While Kurt and Mrs. Shaw moved toward the the street and around to the entrance of the house, Meg held back, pausing a moment to study the coach house and consider its possibilities. Did it need to be torn down? Could it be fixed up as a rental? A guest house?

Suddenly a movement or shadow at an upper window drew her attention. Meg squinted in the sunlight and shaded her eyes.

There behind the filthy glass, Meg was certain, was the face of a child. A little boy and a mist of some kind that was enveloping him. He seemed to stare out at her with unnaturally large, pleading eyes—his visage like some old Renoir portrait—as if to call for help. Yes, the mouth seemed to be moving . . .

The sun blinded Meg for a moment, and she blinked. When she looked again, the image had vanished.

"Meg! Hurry up!" Kurt called. "We're going in!"

Inside the main house, she took the realtor aside. Mrs. Shaw laughed politely, her high platinum hair shifting slightly. "A child? In the coach house? Impossible, my dear. Impossible! I'll tell you the truth, Mrs. Rockwell, the coach house is in falling-down condition, and it's been sealed tighter than an Egyptian tomb. No child would be at play there, I can assure you. It must have been a reflection you saw."

"Yes, I suppose it was," Meg said.

But she knew otherwise.

"Meg!" Kurt was calling from the second floor. "Wait till you see the size of the bathroom up here and the wonderful old fixtures!"

"Coming!" Meg called back.

Later, Meg herself saw the large padlock that secured the entrance to the second floor of the old coach house. As they entered and climbed the long narrow staircase, Mrs. Shaw recounted the building's history. "It started out as a barn. This was all farmland, of course. Then it was used as a garage and charging facility for electric cars. But a fire took it to the ground. It was rebuilt as a coach house and the upstairs here was fitted out with this very quaint little one-bedroom apartment. Unfortunately, the building is no longer sound."

"Will we be able to rent it out—with repairs, of course?" Kurt asked.

Mrs. Shaw shook her head. "The city has declared this a dangerous building. I'm just being honest with you, Mr. Rockwell. And, besides the block is zoned for single families. Any grandfather clause that might have pertained expired long ago."

"I see," Kurt said, lacking the interest of a motivated buyer.

Mrs. Shaw went on talking, pointing out how a large and modern garage might be erected on the site—once the building was razed.

Meg walked into the small bedroom that fronted the house. She looked out the dirty window and down the drive to where she had stood earlier. The image of the child came back to her. She only now recalled that he had been wearing wire-rimmed glasses. Simultaneous with this image came a rush of cold that penetrated every part of her body. She had never felt such a cold.

"This would make a great little apartment, huh, Meg?" Kurt had followed her into the room, startling her. "But don't you think," he whispered, "we're wasting Mrs. Shaw's time?"

As she turned to him, she took a step away from the window. The cold dissipated, almost as if it had moved through her.

"Are you okay?"

"What? Oh, yes, just chilled a bit. Come over here, Kurt. Take a look out the window."

Kurt took Meg's place at the window. "Yeah? Now what?"

"Nothing. I just thought this view of the house was a good one." Kurt had not experienced the cold—that was clear.

"Yeah, it's great architecture all the way around. I'll give you that."

Kurt left the room to check out the little bathroom. "Well, *this* room is hopeless," he called. "The ceiling has fallen in."

Mrs. Shaw appeared in the doorway. "You see? No child. It must have been light and shadows playing tricks on you. Nothing here, Mrs. Rockwell."

Meg smiled. She was not about to press the issue of the little boy. She would have seemed quite the fool to insist that someone had been there. Clearly, no one had lived or played there for many years.

Meg didn't mention it again, certainly not to Kurt. She had already decided that the house was to be theirs and wanted nothing to stand in the way.

She would not admit it to another soul or even to herself, but somewhere, in the smallest, most secret chamber of her heart, Meg knew that she had seen a ghost.

Meg started to leave the little bedroom. Something made her turn around in the doorway. She saw only a dingy room in serious disrepair. At that moment, the cold took her again—possessed her for but fleeting moments—and fell away.

Something had moved through her and out into the hallway. Something not of this world.

TWO

HAMMOND, INDIANA

ON A SATURDAY IN APRIL, at dusk, Meg stood on the second floor balcony of her house on Springfield Street, watching the Allied Van Lines truck pull away, heading east to the Illinois border, just a block away.

The dream had materialized.

Yet a sudden and inexplicable depression gripped her. She felt sick to her stomach, dizzy as she looked down at their tree-lined street. It wasn't the old vertigo—it was a plunging rush of self-doubt, unusual for someone who seldom second-guessed herself in day-to-day situations.

But, like her marriage to Kurt, this was of major import. What have I done, she asked herself. *What have I done?*

She stared out at the old willow tree in the front yard. It and the house were theirs. Kurt had called her insistence in buying it her whim of iron.

She had such whims, she knew.

But was *this* merely a whim? Two doors down a family of four was getting out of their Honda Civic. The woman looked up and gave a little uncertain wave before guiding her little son and daughter into the house. The husband hadn't noticed her. What was life to be like in this great, rambling sixteen-room house?

She stared down the quiet street.

Is this a mistake? Her stomach took on a dull, churning pain. Had Kurt been right in thinking Hammond was too far from their roots? What was it about the house that had prompted her to bully him?

"Hi!"

Meg looked across the street to where two little blond girls stood. They were about six-years-old and clearly identical twins. They waved.

"Hi, yourself!" Meg called, waving. Small children seemed to be a part of the Springfield Street landscape. It would be a good place to raise her child.

The girls giggled and ran away.

She turned now, thankful for the diversion, and moved toward the French doors leading to the sitting room and master bedroom behind it. As she did so, her eyes swept the façade of the coach house, but she did not allow herself time to focus. In their subsequent trips to the house following their first visit with Mrs. Shaw, Meg had carefully avoided the coach house. She had no wish to see that face again, no wish to enter that structure again. Once Kurt's condo was sold and money was more fluid, they would have the coach house bulldozed.

Meg stood just inside the door, her eyes scanning the sitting room, then—visible through open mahogany double doors—the bedroom. Her heart tightened a bit. Furniture, boxes, and bags were everywhere. Any sense of organization had given way to the sheer quantity of things. Not only had things come from the condo, but both she and Kurt had also granted freedom to myriad items in storage—from Kurt's first marriage and from her own collection of antiques and family heirlooms that had crowded her tiny one-bedroom on Halsted Street. The aggregate result was daunting.

Rex, who loved exploring new surroundings and containers of all kinds, pounced happily from one box to another. Meg smiled at

JAMES CONROYD MARTIN

him, took in the whole space again, and sighed at the magnitude of the task ahead of her.

The master plan was to put all the boxes on the second floor while they organized the downstairs rooms. For the time being, they would sleep in a back bedroom on the first floor, one that Mrs. Shaw said had once been the music room. Meg loved the horizontal panel of windows there, made up of clear and frosted leaded glass and green and amber stained glass. She thought the design was Prairie.

The piano, Meg told Kurt, had no doubt been positioned under the bank of windows. How did she know that, he had asked. Meg shrugged, calling it a logical guess.

She did not say that she had been visited with the clearest possible mental image of a polished upright sitting there, the word Steinway in bright gold letters above the keyboard.

Meg didn't allow herself to dwell on the image. She had had such moments before. After her grandmother's passing, she had helped her parents clear out her grandmother's apartment, and she found she could picture in those rooms people and furniture out of the past. She had no idea whether such images had somehow crossed time's threshold or had come from her imagination.

She began to work on sorting through the boxes, tossing the empties down the rear stairway just off the enclosed back porch.

An hour later, Kurt trudged up the front stairs. "The phone is on already."

"Good."

"Made the first phone call, too—the local pizza parlor. I'm starved!"

"I am, too." Meg smiled even though she was silently counting calories. Her waistline was thickening by the minute. She had already gained seven pounds in the first trimester. Seven pounds! But she would eat at least two pieces, three if they weren't too big. She wasn't about to dampen Kurt's enthusiasm. Once he had made the leap, agreeing to buy the house, he began to invest his own

24

enthusiasm in the move—even when the condo hadn't sold and they had the chance to back out of the house deal.

For the time being they had two residences. Things would be tight until the condo sold, especially with her cutting back to a part-time job. Only the day before, Kurt had suggested that he stay at the condo during the week until it sold. Meg didn't like the idea but agreed. After all, it was Kurt who would have to commute by train every day.

"I'll go down and clear a spot for us to eat," Kurt said, kissing Meg on the cheek.

Meg watched him descend the steps. She anticipated—with ambivalence—seeing Kurt off on Monday morning. She would miss him, of course, but she savored the thought of having the house to herself. Why was that? Her mind leapt to a writer who wrote of houses as living entities with powers to welcome, protect, disturb, or alienate. He was English, she knew. She thought hard, but the name eluded her.

Meg studied the twelve-foot-high panel of three stained glass windows that lighted the front staircase. The green and amber shades of the glass were beautiful. It awed her to look at it, filled her with warmth.

Kurt came bounding upstairs again. He grabbed Meg's hand. "Come downstairs, Meg!"

"The pizza couldn't get here that fast!"

"No, it's the buffet! Wait till you see. You'll love it!"

"What?" Meg laughed as he steered her down the stairs, past the windows on the landing. "Does it fit?"

For weeks they had argued in friendly fashion as to whether Meg's grandmother's Empire buffet would fit into the alcove in the dining room. They had measured the buffet and the opening a half dozen times. The opening seemed no wider than the buffet.

Kurt had been pessimistic about its chances. "Just sell it," he joked, "we'll find something else to fit—something maybe in Formica."

Meg had laughed, providing Kurt with a mock slap. But she knew Kurt could sell everything he owned and be content—as long as he had his computer, phone, and briefcase.

Meg gasped now as she came into the dining room. Not only was the buffet snugged neatly into the elegant opening, but its dark oak matched the frames of the three little leaded glass windows high above it. "It fits!" she said. "Oh my God! It really fits!"

"As if it belongs there," Kurt replied. "And there isn't an eighth of an inch to spare, I can tell you!"

"I knew it would fit."

"So you said." Kurt laughed. "But lots of things seem to fit in just so." He stepped aside so that she could see into the half of the double parlor that fronted the dining room. "Take a look there, Lady Rockwell!"

Meg stared in amazement. Kurt had wasted no time. In perfect proportion, her oriental carpet hugged the darkly varnished floor. On either side of the great red brick fireplace sat their two modern leather loveseats, new purchases. Kurt's Aunt Nelly's rocker claimed a corner of the bay. And in the bay's center, on a walnut Eastlake table, sat Meg's most cherished possession: an antique lamp with a base made from a Rookwood vase and an all-glass domed shade, both components handpainted in a vivid blue and purple iris pattern. The glass dome had what one antique dealer termed a chipped ice effect, one that sent fractured slivers of light out into the bay.

Meg walked to the lamp and gently touched the shade. "How beautiful it must be from the street!" she exclaimed.

"Like everything else, it just fits, Meg. I bet that lamp is almost as old as the house."

Meg stopped to think. The lamp had come with a short oral history by way of her mother. Her heart stopped for a moment.

"What is it, Meg? You look odd."

"My grandparents received it for their wedding, Kurt."

"Yeah?—So?"

"Kurt, they were married in 1910."

"Now that's a strange coincidence. The same year the house was built!"

———◦◦◎◦◦———

Meg slept well. Despite their exhaustion, they christened the house with lovemaking.

The bed frame had yet to be assembled, so Meg and Kurt lounged in a bed close to the floor that first morning, playing with Rex. They were in no hurry to get up.

Meg thought how in less than six months—God willing!—they would be playing with their own child. She was at last going to experience birth and motherhood. She would hold her own child in this bed, in this house.

Suddenly, Rex's body became tense, his ears on alert. He bounded out of the room and ran through the hallway to the front of the house.

"What's gotten into the cat?" Meg asked.

"Cats do that, Meg."

"Not Rex so much. It's strange. I'm going to see what he's up to." She was pulling herself up from the low, frameless bed when she heard the sound.

It was a human sound, she was certain, high, tremulous, yet exuberant, exclaiming just once: "Kitty, oooh, kitty!"

Meg stood over the bed, paralyzed, one arm in her robe. "Did you hear that?" she cried, turning to Kurt.

"What?" Kurt was wiping the sleep from his eyes.

"That sound, that voice, didn't you hear it? Kurt, it was a child's voice!"

"Oh, Meg, it was Rex. You know how cats often sound like babies."

Not Rex, Meg wanted to say. She thought better of it.

Instead, she hurried out into the parlor, pulling on her robe as she went.

Rex stood in the middle of the room, staring up at her, the amber eyes huge and his back arched high in fear or caution.

"Everything all right?" Kurt called. "It was probably a neighbor kid outside, Meg."

"Yeah, probably," Meg said. Pulling the robe around herself, she went into the kitchen to scramble eggs.

THREE

T HE TRAIN HAD BEEN ON time: 7:32 a.m. If Kurt resented his first commute, he gave no indication.

Returning home from dropping him off, Meg drove her blue Saturn south on Hohman, through downtown Hammond. It didn't look too bad, she told herself, despite much of what she saw. Stores were nearly extinct, victims of the craze for malls in the 70s and 80s. Empty lots stood where small businesses, theaters, banks, and small hotels once provided a grid of urban activity. Three huge department stores had fallen away to broken shells, corroding in the sun and rain, waiting to be demolished.

Meg did a double take when she passed the old Fred Astaire studio. The traffic light went to red and she braked. She turned her head now and studied the structure. The studio comprised the entire second floor of a block of stores. She looked up to where the tall broken windows of the ballroom allowed for the wind to blow in against the once-elegant, once-red drapes. Nearly every small city had its Fred Astaire Studio, she thought, in a happier era, before changing times and insolvency. What had become of those armies of people who mamboed, fox-trotted, and waltzed their way through the post-war period? Damn few were still dancing. Not even Fred himself.

Is there dancing on the other side? Meg laughed out loud at the whimsical thought. The light flashed green and Meg stepped on the gas, putting the thought and studio behind her.

According to Mrs. Shaw, there was hope for Hammond. The mayor had initiated a program to attract white collar businesses, to some success. A Thai restaurant just recently opened and seemed to be doing well. Incredibly, hardware and plumbing supply stores had survived on the sheer tenacity of their octogenarian owners. One of the local banks had just opened a branch adjacent to and within blocks of the house on Springfield Street, and a new Federal courthouse had just been built.

Meg put the car in gear, driving past St. Margaret Mercy, a Hammond anchor for a century. She wondered how social work was addressed there, then put it out of her mind. She was through with hospital social work. She longed for the freedom of part-time social work in home care. The interview the week before had gone extremely well, and Meg knew the job was hers even before the call came two days later.

At her own request, she was not to begin her job for two weeks, and she looked forward to the interim as a bit of a vacation in which she would settle into the house and into a decidedly slow Hammond pace.

It would be a luxury, too, to leave Liz Claiborne hanging in the closet. Slacks and wash and wear blouses would be the order of the day for house calls, jeans and sweats for home.

Meg was home in seven minutes flat.

She found Rex curled up on the cushion of the rocker, sunshine from the bay washing over him. "Well, you've certainly made yourself at home," she told him, stroking under his jaw, withdrawing her hand quickly when he attempted a playful bite.

She picked him up, scolding him in a light-hearted way. She carried Rex as she surveyed the house now, room by room. She looked at the rug, the buffet, the lamp. Everywhere, it seemed, the house welcomed her. She felt more than a peace here—she felt a kind of subtle euphoria. She would have her child here. She would be happy here. It was home.

Meg was to have the house to herself for five days. She felt more than a flicker of guilt that she was looking forward to these days without Kurt. *Is this normal?* But her time was soon taken up with unpacking, sorting, and organizing. He'll be here on a regular basis soon enough, she told herself.

The day passed quickly, mostly in the kitchen. If it were true that kitchens sold houses, this house would still have been on the market. It was a galley kitchen, meant not for the original family but for the servants who prepared and served the family's meals. Meg thought a new floor and light fixtures and several coats of paint would breathe fresh life into the room. After the new refrigerator arrived from Sears, Meg went to the supermarket and bought enough to fill it, as well as the large walk-in pantry.

At night she carefully secured the four entrances on the ground floor, as Kurt had done the first nights and as he had cautioned her to do. The front door had the standard key lock, but Meg noticed that it also had a hook and eye lock. Extra security, she thought, as she attempted to guide the hook into the eye—but the two would not connect. It seemed as if the doorframe—or the house itself—had settled, throwing the hook out of alignment with the eye. Determined, she struggled and struggled with it until the undersides of her right hand became red and sore. She gave up at last, telling herself the extra security was not needed.

She fell into bed that night exhausted. Before falling off to sleep—which came quickly—she cautioned herself against such strenuous activity in the future. This was her first pregnancy, and she had to remember that she was thirty-seven years old. The house was important, but not nearly so much as the child, her child. She started to think of possible names, but she had scarcely considered a few girls' names when sleep came, sometime before eleven.

At one a.m. Meg came suddenly awake.

She lay there, curious about what had awakened her. Something had, she knew. Had Rex jumped onto or off the bed? She looked down to the foot of the bed. The streetlight in the alley sent a diffused multi-textured light through the stained glass panels above her head. Rex was still there at the foot of the bed, seemingly in the same position as at bedtime. And Meg knew his habits, too: he was not the nocturnal type and often slept the whole night on the queen-size bed.

Rex was staring back at Meg with wide, bewildered eyes. Was there fear in them?

Meg lay back and listened.

Nothing.

She turned on her side now, settling in for sleep.

And she was nearly asleep when she heard it.

A light tapping. Three or four times.

Instinctively, she reached up behind her head, thinking the headboard was too close to the wall.

She realized her mistake immediately when her knuckles struck the plaster wall. The headboard had not been attached yet; the box spring and mattress still sat flush on the floor.

What was it then?

Tap . . . tap . . . tap . . . tap.

Fear threatened to rise up within her, but Meg held it down. The noise seemed to be coming from within the wall; however, she would not believe it. She got up, fully awake now, and peered out the window, thinking—hoping—that it was a tree branch or a cable lashing against the wood siding of the house. Something.

She could see nothing.

Was it a wire rattling within the old wall? Kurt had said the old wiring was still in place and would have to be replaced. Or perhaps an old gas pipe had come loose. The house had been erected during a time when both gas and electric were used for lighting, especially in the houses of the wealthy.

Tap . . . tap . . . tap . . . tap.

Meg put her ear to the wall.

Was it a mouse? No—mice *scratched* within walls. They didn't tap.

Meg could see that the hair on Rex's back was standing straight up. He stood up now, his back humped high.

The cat sensed something—what? Meg shivered as a chill rippled through her.

Tap . . . tap . . . tap . . . tap.

Rex meowed in a kind of whine, jumped, and ran from the room.

Meg's inclination was to run, too. But she stayed and her initial fear gave way to irritation. The tapping stopped, but it was an hour before she was able to fall back to sleep.

Then, at four a.m., there came another cluster of tapping. Meg lay there unmoving, awake but with eyes closed. She told herself that ignoring them made them less real. Within the half hour, they ceased. Just the same, she didn't sleep the rest of the night.

As she unpacked and cleaned the next day—her body tired and mind cloudy—she tried not to think of the tapping, its source or meaning, if meaning it had. She didn't tell Kurt about it when he called. She tried to think of other things—things that needed doing, her parents' reaction to the house, caring for a newborn.

In the afternoon she went to collect the newspaper from the front porch. Passing through the one heavy mullioned door into the vestibule, she undid the lock and tugged at the matching front door. It didn't budge. She couldn't figure it. Was it stuck? Her gaze moved up now, above her eye level, and she saw that the hook had been neatly placed into the eye.

She stood stunned for what must have been a full minute before she attempted to dislodge the hook. She was unsuccessful; it held fast. She went to find a hammer and one quick upward swing did the trick. She would not use the lock again. The house, it seemed, had an abundance of mysteries.

On Tuesday, despite her exhausted state, Meg was nervous with anticipation and couldn't get to sleep. One a.m. came and went without incident. She breathed a sigh of relief and eventually fell asleep—but not before suddenly remembering what writer it was who wrote about houses that possessed personalities and powers all their own. It was E. M. Forster in his masterpiece *Howards End*. She had done a paper on it in a college British Lit. class.

———————⦿———————

At three a.m. precisely, however, she was awakened by the same four-tap clusters. She lay there listening, her heart pounding with a mix of emotions. Fear. Desperation. Anger. And the paralyzing thought that buying the house had been an impulsive mistake—that she should have listened to Kurt.

Tap . . . tap . . . tap . . . tap.

She could not help but think that someone, something, was making a fool of her. Someone was watching her! She sensed it. Her mind was in a ferment. *What is happening? Who or what is doing this?*

She tried not to move.

The tapping stopped—only to resume at five a.m.

Meg got through Wednesday by keeping busy and trying not to think about the coming night. Every fiber, every cell within her, communicated that something uncanny and terrible had only just begun. For everything that she unpacked, she feared that she would be repacking it all too soon. Was it possible that the house that had seemed to welcome her was now turning against her?

Had it not been for her pregnancy, Meg would have taken a sleeping pill Wednesday night. The measure turned out to be unnecessary, though. She was so physically and emotionally spent that she did fall asleep, sometime before midnight.

Meg's radio alarm went off at seven a.m.

Her eyes opened, testing the light. There had been no noise, she was certain. She had slept soundly though the night. Sighing in relief, she rose and went about preparing a good breakfast. She dared to hope she had heard the last of the foreign sounds.

The tapping did not come on Thursday, either. Meg had given herself over to a deep, confident slumber. In the morning she luxuriated in a kind of half-sleep.

Eventually, the strains of music penetrated her consciousness. The sounds of a piano. She reached over to press the ten-minute snooze alarm. As she opened her eyes, she suddenly realized that the room was fully dark and that the clock read five-ten, not seven a.m., the time she had set.

As her sleepy mind attempted to grasp this fact, she realized something else: the music did not stop when she pressed the snooze button.

Her eyes opened wide now and she pulled the radio to her ear, knocking a glass of water to the floor in the process.

The piano music was *not* coming from the radio.

Terrified, immobile, Meg could only listen.

The music—something familiar and light and at low volume—Debussey?—seemed to be coming from within the wall behind Meg's head.

Yes, she knew this piece. It was Debussey's *LeMer*.

Kurt's train, the 6:20, was several minutes late. Extra minutes of nervous anticipation before it finally arrived. Meg breathed deeply as she saw Kurt sight the car, then wave. At the Chicago condo, he had changed from his typical dark suit to khaki dockers and a blue chambray shirt.

She prayed that he would see no change in her. If I am careful, she thought, watching his six-foot frame lope toward the Saturn, he won't notice anything amiss. God bless him, he's not the type to notice.

Meg had decided not to tell Kurt anything. She would let fate chart the course.

One of two things would happen. Either the phenomenon would continue, and Kurt would bear witness to it himself—or it would cease—yet, if it did, for how long?

If only it were some aberration that would not recur. Ever.

"Hi!" Kurt was beaming as he folded his legs into the passenger seat. "Boy, what a week! Am I ready for a slow weekend in Hammond!"

"Is that something like a slow waltz in Cedar Bend?"

"Huh? Is that a book or something?" He leaned over and kissed Meg.

She laughed. "Never mind."

"Another literary allusion of yours? You should have been an English teacher."

" Yes, it was an allusion, but not very literary, I'm afraid. And maybe I will teach—down the line."

"Wouldn't surprise me. What's to eat? I'm starved. They had overcooked cod in the cafeteria today, and I couldn't eat it."

"I haven't exactly been tied to the kitchen—no, I take that back. I have—but not with food. Mostly cleaning and stocking the shelves. We'll eat out if that's okay."

"What choice do I have?" he asked, reaching over and squeezing her knee.

They drove to a well-recommended Chinese restaurant in nearby Calumet City. The Szechwan entrees were perfect. Meg, in keeping with her condition, ordered a moderately zesty chicken and pea pods dish rather than one of her extra hot selections. Predictably, Kurt ordered his Egg Foo Young, which he proclaimed the best he ever had. He was in a chatty mood and brought her up on hospital politics.

Meg could not enjoy her food and his hospital anecdotes were more annoying than interesting. She unconsciously tuned him out and found herself thinking about what she had been through—and what the night might bring.

If the tapping or music recurs, how will Kurt take it? she wondered. Will there be a fight? How angry will he be that I didn't tell him about the occurrences immediately?

And that face! Thought of the pale face at the coach house window on the first day gave her a start. Will Kurt forgive me that even then I was certain that someone—something—lurked in the coach house?

A thought occurred to Meg now that she had been holding at bay all day: What if there was some connection between the recent happenings and the coach house apparition? The thought brought up gooseflesh on her arms and destroyed her appetite. She told herself that there was not some entity within their new home—but with little conviction.

"What's wrong, Meg?"

"What do you mean?"

"You went a bit pale."

"Did I? This is a lot spicier than I expected."

"Well, let's send it back."

"No, I'm quite full, anyway."

She watched Kurt across the table, imagining ways in which she—or the house itself—might reveal the—what? Paranormal?—events to him. It took little imagination to know that he would demand that they move out at once.

The thought of losing the house cut through to her heart. Despite the tapping, the piano music, the child's face, and her fear of whatever was behind these things, she realized that she was not about to give up the house. Her guess was that many people would not have lasted the week, yet she was prepared to dig in.

Her pregnancy gave her pause, however. She had hoped to carry the child in a healthy and stress-free environment. Was that going to be possible?

Kurt finished his meal, talking at some length about the business of running a hospital, the necessaries of running a business, things that already seemed distant, unimportant, and dull to Meg. She listened absently, and her hesitation about the child passed in deference to her attachment to the house. The bond to the house was mysterious but strong as steel.

She could only wonder about and fear Kurt's reaction when it all came out.

At home, Kurt approved of the refrigerator and went on to rave about the kitchen. "You've managed to find a place for everything in this tiny space. It's a damned miracle, Meg. It looks like a real kitchen."

"The floor is no miracle, Kurt. This 70s linoleum is crap."

"Okay, new floor. I'll start a list."

"Good!"

"But tomorrow you cook, sweetie pie."

"Fine, just drop the sweetie pie crap. I'll cook. Something nice and fattening. How about lasagna?"

"Lasagna on Saturday night. For that I'd submit to a night of blissful bondage." He gave Meg a good-natured pinch.

"You're bad." Meg laughed. "But bondage here may not be very blissful."

"What?"

"Nothing." *Good God*, she thought. What had made her say that?

"Another allusion? Okay, I got it! Something to do with Of Human Bondage? By . . . by – "

"Somerset Maughan."

"Yeah!"

"No."

"Shit!" Kurt looked crestfallen. "What, then?"

Meg shrugged. She thought *Amityville Horror*, but didn't voice it. "Sorry. No allusion."

When Friday night passed without incident, Meg dared to

become cautiously elated. A part of her brain tried to convince her that it had been her imagination all along. She didn't buy it, of course, but prayed that it *had* been only an aberration.

On Saturday Meg and Kurt worked on putting the first floor in order. During the week Meg had mentally positioned every chair, table, floor lamp, and now she took advantage of Kurt's help in actually placing each piece. She rewarded him by cooking. Their initial formal meal in the dining room, complete with flowers and candles—and her best lasagna—went well.

Meg found herself trembling when it came time to go to bed. Two nights without incident was too much to expect. The moment of truth was at hand, and she lay in bed, waiting for Kurt and worried more about his reaction to the occurrences than she did the occurrences themselves.

Kurt brought two candles into the room, placed them on the dresser, and climbed into bed.

"What's this?" he asked.

"What?"

"This!" he said.

"It's called a nightgown. I was chilled."

"Well, I'll warm you up. No nightgowns on the weekend. That'll be the rule—at least as long as I'm in the city during the week."

Kurt buried his face in Meg's shoulder and neck, his mouth moving to her ear then her mouth. His kiss was warm and welcome.

Pulling away slightly, he said, "Take it off, Meg."

Meg obeyed. Slowly, she gave herself over to Kurt and her own desire.

Kurt fell asleep first, and she, too, fell into a sound sleep by midnight.

Again, no occurrences.

<hr />

Kurt and Meg drove to Sunday brunch at an old roadhouse in Union Pier, a Michigan/Indiana border town now reenergized by a younger generation. Returning, they spent a slow, relaxing day at home, doing little real work, and taking an afternoon walk through the neighborhood.

Sunday night made for turnabout and Kurt cooked. Salad, pork chops, baked potatoes, and green beans. Meg was effusive in her compliments, thankful for the way they were interacting, content in the mundane details of living a quiet existence with someone. She would miss Kurt come Monday, she realized.

They retired early.

When morning came—again without drama—Meg charged into the day with her old enthusiasm. After returning from dropping Kurt at the train station, she started taking apart the upstairs, room by room, box by box. In the afternoon she went to the River Oaks Shopping Center and did some shopping for the baby's room, stopping at the Marshall Field's coffee shop to treat herself to decaffeinated coffee and a delectable pasta salad. Full of mayonnaise, she thought, but what the hell, it's worth every ounce I'll have to carry—and shed later.

In the evening, Meg had to consciously slow her pace, forcing herself to sit and watch some old post-war Ingrid Bergman film on the Classics cable network.

She went to bed before it ended and fell promptly asleep, tired and happy. She felt that there would be no tapping, no music, because she willed it so.

And so it was. No tapping. No piano music. Was it some kind of psychic premonition? Or had she willed the occurrences out of existence?

But on that April spring night, the dreams began.

FOUR

M EG FOUND HERSELF WALKING DOWN an unfamiliar street,
her eyes cast down. She watched mesmerized as her
voluminous skirt, dark and heavy, moved forward by the thrust of
her legs, then back.

Forward, then back.

The air was hot and wet with humidity. The skirt was
cumbersome, too, and she began to feel flushed, then faint.

Still, she watched the skirt move, as if by a mechanical motion.

Could this be *her* skirt? It was so long! Why, she could not see
her legs, or even her ankles! Only her shoes, shoes she had never
seen before, more like boots they were, fastened to her feet by
rows of buttons.

Meg watched as if through a kind of tunnel vision over which
she had no control. She was unable to lift her head or turn it to
see around her.

Her pace accelerated.

She moved as if she were in some terrible hurry, as if she were
running from something, or someone. Faster and still faster—
what was the rush? Why couldn't she slow down? She felt as if
she were about to fall, as if the slightest misstep would send her
sprawling onto ground.

Where was she going?

Her feet passed over bricked squares, then hard earth, bricks then earth. She walked, it seemed, for miles—yet her camera-like vision recorded no progress.

She heard a din of traffic, voices, activity. But her line of vision seemed locked in a downward perspective.

Meg pressed on despite the heat, despite her fatigue—not because she wanted to—but because she was being drawn—against her will—away from or toward something. She was no more than a marionette.

At last, a clue. A paper flyer lay at her feet. She was past it in seconds, however, without having had the time to focus on it. Why couldn't she look around her? Why couldn't she stop?

Then she saw the white of another flyer. Of the many words printed upon it, she had time only to focus on the largest block letters. It read:

DE WOLF HOPPER
A MATINEE IDOL

And then it was gone.

Suddenly, Meg became aware of a pressure in her right hand. Something was pulling, tugging violently at her, as if to wrench itself free.

She realized now that it was a hand, a small—yet extremely strong—hand. She struggled to hold on to it. The hand squirmed vigorously in hers.

It was a child's hand.

Fear flooded into her, as if a sluice gate had opened, filling her with one thought: she must not lose that hand! That child!

Yet she did lose it. Despite her viselike grip, the hand slipped from hers as if it were no longer of material substance.

Meg could not see anything, but she sensed the child moving away from her, moving out into a vast, foggy void.

She reached out to grasp the hand, but her own came up empty. She opened her mouth to call the child. The scream was silent.

And what name would she have called? She had no idea.

The realization that she had lost something loved and precious came over her like the resounding lid of a stone coffin.

Meg felt her own life being stifled, choked, ended.

She called out some name as unfamiliar to her as the street and her clothing.

No reply.

She called again.

As she inhaled breath to call yet again, she took a single step and felt herself falling, plunging into some huge expanse of space. The vertigo of a thousand childhood nightmares set her stomach roiling, rushed at her face with dry, dangerous breaths.

Then she saw the outlines of rectangular objects flying up at her in one formation.

Bricks?

Yes, bricks. The bricked crossing of the street was flying up to meet her!

Meg opened her mouth to scream.

Suddenly, she came awake. She lay there for nearly an hour, wide awake and consumed with an enormous sense of loss, an emotion that would recur throughout the day.

And she had the oddest feeling that she had left her body during that dream.

In the morning Meg called Denise Clooney, a social worker and entrepreneur who supplied hospitals and agencies with social workers who served as temps, per diem, or by assignment. Denise was Meg's new employer.

Meg carefully recorded the names and numbers of three people—two elderly women and a handicapped man in his fifties—who were to be her first patients. All three would be released from the hospital at the end of the week. It was Meg's responsibility to make initial homecare calls to determine the needs of each—meals, nursing, prescriptions, physical or psychological therapy.

Cut and dried. Easy stuff for a woman of Meg's experience. Meg called the relatives of each and set up appointments for the following week. By lunchtime her work schedule for the coming week was in place.

She had had no breakfast but still had no appetite. Nonetheless, she could not fast in her condition and so forced down a cheese sandwich and a half bowl of tomato soup. Comfort food that brought no comfort. Her business done and lunch eaten, her thoughts returned to the dream. She could ignore it no longer. It was strange—usually she could not remember her dreams, but today she had had full recall upon awakening. Its images kept returning at unpredictable moments, too, chilling her.

Did the dream have meaning? She could not help but think that it did. But what meaning?

The dream, in every disturbing and haunting detail, recurred on Tuesday, again in the morning just before dawn.

Meg awoke in a sweat.

Why had she been dressed in heavy clothing that closed tightly at her throat and draped to her toes. What was this place of bricked street crossings and hard earth? What was the significance of this dream?

And what was this terrible fear that came over her as she tried to hold on to the phantom child? This brooding sense of loss when the hand slipped away? What was going to happen to the nameless, faceless child who had pulled away and run from her? What terrible thing?

Meg's hands moved down to her slightly rounded belly as one fear transmuted into another.

Was the dream some subconscious premonition or psychic foreknowledge? Was *her* child in danger? From what? Whom? Would she lose her child? Her heart pumped blood to her head at the thought. Her temples pulsed, and she felt faint.

44

When the dream came for a third time, on Wednesday, it came with a difference. This time it seemed as if she not only lived the dream—the clothes of another era, the heat, a child's hand, panic and horror—but she also simultaneously observed the dream from an objective viewpoint.

Meg slept, yet she was aware that she was dreaming. How was this possible? As if from above, she could *see* herself, lying on her back in the bed, her face placid, her eyes closed. She had never heard of such a thing. But it was true and it was happening to her in the here and now. Without time to consider this further, the film-like dream took her, and she began to look for details she had been unable to notice previously.

She noticed at once that some dark oily substance seemed to coat the hard earth of the street. The liquid had spattered her shoes, stained the hem of her long dress as if with ink. What is it? she wondered. What had been spilled?

Then, at her feet, she saw the white flyer with its black lettering. This time, however, her own awareness that she was dreaming somehow allowed her to slow the dream's pace, gaining the time needed to study the words again. She read:

TOWLE OPERA HOUSE
DE WOLF HOPPER
A MATINEE IDOL
THE FUNNIEST COMEDY OF THE SEASON.

Then it was gone and the dream concluded in the same terrifying way: the hand pulling away, the dreadful realization that something precious—a child—was being ripped from her grasp forever.

———————◦◦◦◦◦———————

At 10:00 a.m., her half-eaten cereal in the sink, Meg dialed the number of Wenonah Smythe.

45

Wenonah was a bright, mildly manic woman two years younger than Meg. They had met ten years before, when Meg had only just begun her career at Ravensfield and Wenonah was fresh out of the hospital's nursing school. They became the closest of friends, and when Meg chose her as maid of honor, her parents hadn't blinked an eye that she had chosen a black woman. Only Aunt Geri Louise registered real surprise, her thin-lipped mouth falling open. Wenonah still worked at Ravensfield, in ER.

Although Wenonah lived in a roomy condo in the Pattington directly across the street from the Rockwell condo, Meg had seen much less of Wenonah after the marriage. Meg thought Kurt was the reason. Kurt was one subject about which the loquacious Wenonah seldom spoke. Why was she so cool toward him?

Was Wenonah jealous that Meg's relationship with Kurt was a successful one, while her own five-year affair with a French doctor had ended in disaster? Was she jealous of the new demands on Meg's time? Was there something about Kurt that she disliked? Kurt always spoke well of Wenonah.

After the phone rang four times, Wenonah's machine picked up.

Meg left a brief message asking her to call back. She hung up, hoping her voice had sounded normal.

Meg did her best to busy herself. There was still plenty to be done, but the joy of starting a new life in what seemed a wonderful old home had been washed away, superseded by insecurity and tension.

She dared not use the vacuum on the steps or on the upper floor, which was fully carpeted, for fear that she wouldn't hear the phone.

A few minutes after noon, Wenonah Smythe rang back.

FIVE

M<small>EG'S HEART SWELLED IN RELIEF</small> when she saw Wenonah through the double set of eight-foot doors, each with four vertical panes of beveled glass. It was only 1:15. She must have dropped everything and pressed her white Datsun to the limit.

When Meg pulled open the second heavy door, Wenonah's eyes were wide as wheels.

"Good Lord, Margaret Rockwell!" she exclaimed. "How did you find this house? Mansion, I should say. The pillars are incredible. A damn mansion!"

Meg welcomed her in with a tight smile and a hug.

"Maybe I should've gone round back?"

"Around back?"

"Yeah!" Wenonah was in the entry hall now, eyeing the double parlor. "Your neighbors will think I'm the hired help. Is this antebellum, or what?"

"Hardly." Meg laughed. She was being cheered already. "It's practically a baby—1910. It's Greek Revival with a dash of Federal—or so we were told."

"Revival, huh? Just the same, people who owned these kinds of houses years ago owned people like me."

"Oh, for heaven's sake, Wenonah!" Embarrassed, Meg laughed and shook her head. She had always been surprised by Wenonah's humor, humor that often couched barbs of some sort. Truthful barbs.

"Just donna go aksin' me to fetch no mint juleps, ya hear?" Wenonah had a talent for shifting her speech from one that reflected the highest education to one that took on the voice, tone, grammar, and raised emotional level of the country or street. She knew exactly how to play the contrast. Selective coding, Meg had heard it called.

"I'll take care not to. Enough of that. Come on. The coffee's ready."

Wenonah demanded an immediate tour.

Meg obliged, taking her through every room, downstairs first, then upstairs. They finished in the sitting room of the master bedroom. Wenonah was appropriately impressed.

"Let's stay up here to chat," Meg said. "There's so much more light up here, and it's so gray today. I'll bring up the coffee." She left Wenonah staring through the French doors that opened onto the horseshoe-shaped balcony that extended along the full front of the house, then along the sides of the structure.

When Meg returned with the coffee, Wenonah seemed to be watching her every move, her elbows on the arms of the floral platform rocker, her hands supporting her chin.

Meg placed the cups on a tray table, then sat in a cushioned chair across from her friend.

"Okay, girlfriend," Wenonah said, "out with it. What is it? Who is it? What little freckle has marred your paradise? You should be happy as clams here."

Meg nervously reached for her decaffeinated coffee. "Is it that obvious? Am I that transparent?"

"Transparent? Honey, your voice on the phone was transparent! Why do you think I got here so fast?"

"Because you drive like a Chicago cab driver? Always have."

"True—guilty as charged. But I drove even faster today. My old Datsun will never die."

Meg smiled weakly, sipped at her coffee. She had tried to be casual about inviting Wenonah to Hammond without notice. Failing that, she worried now over what to say.

Meg brought her eyes up to Wenonah's questioning dark eyes, suddenly completely humorless. Meg realized that even in her rare serious moments, Wenonah was a strikingly beautiful woman. Perfectly coifed short hair, rounded face, good features, and rich cocoa complexion. Just jeans and a red blouse today, but she could dress well, too.

"I'm listening, Meg."

A grateful sigh went up within Meg. Wenonah knew instinctively what the moment called for. Meg sat forward in her chair and began her story, telling in detail of the face at the coach house window, the tappings, the piano music, the dreams.

Wenonah listened attentively, her face impassive. Asking only occasionally for a clarification, she made no comments, no jokes.

Meg finished, and her sigh was audible this time. A sigh of relief. She had been able to tell her story to someone. Wenonah might have no advice to offer her, she realized, but just the telling and Wenonah's listening—serious listening—had buoyed her considerably.

"Wow," Wenonah said, with more breath than voice.

Meg's heart caught for a moment. "You think I'm crazy!"

"No!" Wenonah's denial was immediate.

"You believe me? You don't think I'm stressed out or something?—Crazy?"

"No. Although we've both been in the medical profession too long, honey, not to come unhinged once in a while." Wenonah reached over and took Meg's hand. "No, I don't think you're crazy."

"That's a relief."

"Yeah, that's the good news."

"But what about the dreams in which I know I am asleep and I'm going through the motions as if I'm a third party observing me?"

49

"Ah, I get those, too."

"You do?"

Wenonah nodded. "Some call them lucid dreams."

"They have a name?"

"Yes, and after a while the dreamer may find that she can manipulate things of her own power. The first time was when my granny died. I was just five, but it was a tragic event in my life. She was closer to me than my mother. The night before the funeral, she came and sat on the side of my bed. I saw her and I saw myself lying there asleep. She soothed me and somehow communicated with me—without words. As she was about to leave, I picked up a small figurine of a ballerina that she had loved and I gave it to her. I just plucked it out of thin air. Go figure."

Meg gave out with a little gasp. "The real figurine?"

"No, of course not, but don't you see, within the dream I could choose what I wished to do. I could cause things to appear. And these lucid dreams have happened a few other times, too, and always at critical moments in my life."

"But this isn't a traumatic time for me—or it shouldn't be. It should be a happy time. New beginnings and all that."

Wenonah cocked her head. "The music, the tapping—not traumatic?"

Meg shrugged, beaten. "Touché."

Wenonah laughed.

"And the bad?" Meg asked.

"The bad?"

"Yeah, you said the good news is that I'm not bonkers—so what's the bad?"

Wenonah released Meg's hand. "Now it's only my opinion, mind you, but I think what we've—no, what *you've* got here is a spirit."

Meg's mouth went dry. She studied her friend. "You do?" Despite the fear that filled her heart, her mood lifted. That Wenonah believed gave her validation, and she could now admit it to herself. "Oh, Wenonah, I know I do! And I can't tell you what it does for me to hear you say so."

"But it's hardly an idyllic situation, is it?"

"No." Meg gasped. "God, no!"

"I take it you didn't return the tapping?"

"Huh? No, I never thought to. . . . Why?"

"Well, you know I'm a talk show junkie. I've seen just about all of the shows that address this sort of stuff . . . you know, the paranormal. It doesn't make me an expert, but I know that tapping is one of the common ways ghosts attempt to establish contact."

"Really?"

Wenonah nodded. "Sometimes a code is worked out and they will answer your questions."

"Well, I'm glad I ignored it then. I don't have any questions I would want to ask it."

"Of course, you do!"

"You mean why it's here. I haven't been in Hammond so long I need to resort to chatting with specters, thank you very much."

Wenonah let go her throaty, infectious laugh. "Hammond can't be that bad."

"No, I'm joking, although Kurt was reticent about setting down roots here. But I can't tell you how much I love this house, how I seem to fit right in—except for this . . . what? . . . phenomenon!"

"That word fits, I guess." Wenonah's eyes narrowed. "Are you avoiding the other word?"

"Ghost?"

"Yeah, ghost."

"Maybe I am."

"How strong do you feel, Meg?"

"Strong enough not to run away after a week. I fully intend to have my baby here!"

"Then do it, Meg. To hell with the damn ghost! Besides, it doesn't seem to be a malevolent one."

"Malevolent?"

"Yeah, like a poltergeist."

"Wait a minute, Win, what's the difference?"

Wenonah furrowed her brow. "I've heard a hundred theories, all different. But many consider ghosts to be the spirits of dead people and that poltergeists are disturbances that draw energy from the living who are sometimes called *mediums*."

"Which is this?"

Wenonah shrugged. "Don't look at me, Meg. I said I ain't no expert. But the two are not totally dissimilar to one another. They both draw energy. That's why you got the cold sensation. They both might start small, like the tapping you heard."

"Or the music?" Meg swallowed hard. "Are you implying they get *bolder* in what they do?"

Wenonah attempted a smile. "Perhaps."

"But how . . . if it keeps acting out . . . And if Kurt— "

"Wait a minute, girl!" Wenonah's eyes went wide. "You mean Kurt hasn't experienced anything?"

Meg cast her eyes down and shook her head.

"And you haven't told him?"

"No."

"Oh, Meg!"

"I know, I know. It's just that my whim got us here in the first place. And I'm not sure that he'll believe me as readily as you have."

"You're right there. He is a little light on the soul side."

"What does that mean?"

"Sorry, nothing offensive. Just that he deals best with things in three dimensions."

"Oh, I guess you're right. I would want him to believe me, but on the other hand, if he does, I'm afraid he'll insist on selling the house."

Wenonah clucked her tongue. "You're going to have to take the chance. Meg, you'll have to trust in him a bit, yes?"

Meg didn't answer.

"Meg, you can't carry this yourself!"

"I know." Meg forced a laugh. "That's why I called you, *girlfriend*."

"Me? Good god! What can I do?"

"I don't know. Give me advice?"

"Look at me, Meg." Wenonah's voice deepened. "Good. Okay, here it is. Tell Kurt. Everything, do you hear? That's the first of two pieces of advice I have for you."

Meg shrank back in her chair. "Tell him about seeing the face in the window before we bought? Oh my God, he'll kill me."

"Then you can truly see the secrets of the other side. Listen, Meg, I don't see how you can be selective about it. The truth's the truth. You've got to tell him."

"Shit."

"Well, excuse me, Margaret Flaherty Rockwell from the school of the good sisters, what did you say?"

"Shit."

"Why, I'm shocked!"

"Don't mess with me, Wenonah. This is serious. . . . What is your other gem of advice, pray tell? Pack up?"

"Well, after you've rinsed the soap out of your foul mouth, I want you to get yourself to the library. I'm sure Hammond has a library—yes?"

"Well, yes, I guess so."

"See what you can find out."

"Find out?"

"About Hammond, about the house, its former residents, the past. And maybe that flyer in your dream! That's something very specific. It may be a creation of your imagination but, you know, opera houses were fairly numerous years ago."

"The library—of course!"

Wenonah shrugged and stood to take her leave. "Merely talk show trivia I've picked up."

"I should have thought of that."

Meg stood and they were starting for the stairs when Wenonah turned to Meg. "I lied—there's one more bit of advice I have."

"What is it?"

"It's fear, Meg, fear. You can't let it in. It will take over."

Meg nodded, sighed. "You know, the dream, that's the strangest part, Win, the dream. I get the sense that I'm dreaming, over and over, someone else's dream, another woman's dream."

"Holy cannoli, Meg. You didn't tell me that."

"Well, it's true. I'm dreaming someone else's dream. I'm sure of it!"

"Christ!—Or you've tapped into her *life*!"

"Her life?" Meg asked. Wenonah had delivered the word like a slap. Meg grasped her friend by the wrist, preventing her from descending the steps. "Have you ever heard of anything like that?"

"No, honey, that's a puzzle for the experts," Wenonah admitted, her dark fathomless eyes fastening on Meg. "Christ Almighty!"

SIX

WENONAH SMYTHE ABSENTMINDEDLY DODGED BOTH Monday's afternoon traffic and the lake wind on Irving Park Road as she dashed toward the White Hen Pantry in the Lake Park Plaza building. The brutally cold wind whipped in off the lake—just a block away—and was sometimes strong enough to knock a person down. Wenonah took it in stride.

She was again thinking about Meg. The visit the previous Thursday had been an upsetting one. She had never seen her friend quite so—vulnerable. If only she and Kurt had not bought a house, if only they had stayed at Lake Park Plaza. Or, better, bought something larger at the Pattington.

The warmth of the little convenience store was a blessed relief. Wenonah shopped here only in an emergency, such as the weather today. The prices were too high. She found it inconvenient to pay the price of convenience. Her grandmother had taught her well how to pinch a penny. Wenonah still clipped coupons and went to a three-dollar second-run movie house.

Just the same, she was a familiar face here because the store had a Cash Station, an attraction that drew her like a gumball machine had once done.

The store was busy. Wenonah made a bee line for the cash station machine. Only one person was ahead of her. An old white man stood working the device as if it were a slot machine that refused to pay off. A minute or two passed as his difficulties in mastering the system increased.

Wenonah watched as his face colored slightly. She tried to remain patient, absently watching the bald head glow hotly under the fluorescent lighting.

Suddenly a voice pierced her consciousness. A voice she recognized.

Kurt Rockwell's.

Wenonah turned about to see him at the tiny deli and sandwich counter and was about to call out a greeting—no one had ever accused her of being shy—when she realized that he was in conversation with a woman.

Wenonah stared for a moment.

A blonde. Shapely, animated. Expensive coat. Educated. Beautiful. Wenonah was adept at immediate assessments. Working in ER at Ravensfield had taught her.

She turned back to the machine. The old man was finally finishing up.

Meg strained to hear the conversation. It was light, something about cheeses and wine, it seemed. She tried to discern the tone. Was this pleasant, pass-the-time counter conversation? Or did he know her? Neighbor? She was not a fellow worker—Wenonah knew everyone at the hospital.

Or are they here together?

Wenonah froze at the thought.

The old man turned around now and apologized for having taken so long, launching into a convoluted story of what he had been doing wrong and admonishing Wenonah not to make the same mistake.

Wenonah smiled solicitously, suppressing her desire to tell the old geezer that she could probably take the machine apart and put it back together. The fool was keeping her from hearing the conversation at the deli counter. She wanted to reach out and grab one of his jug ears and send him toward the door.

Simultaneously, she wondered whether Kurt had seen her. Had the old man brought her to his attention?

Or is the blonde too riveting?

The man was finally leaving. Wenonah stepped up to the machine. She would take her sweet time.

She inserted her card, entered her code. She paused then, listening, trying to fasten on the voices on the other side of the aisle.

Presently she heard steps behind her. She turned around.

A woman stood behind her, waiting for the machine. Wenonah managed a thin smile, then turned back.

Damn!

Wenonah lengthened her stay at the machine by selecting several unneeded transactions. As she played for time, she thought she could hear the woman behind her periodically sighing. Too bad, she thought, at least she didn't have Chuckles the Clown in front of her.

She finished up now. Turning around, she saw that Kurt had his back to her. His words were muffled. Was he trying to be as inconspicuous as possible? Had he caught on to her presence? Was he avoiding her?

Wenonah quickly left the White Hen. She recrossed Irving Park Road, hurrying into the west courtyard of the Pattington. In her vestibule, she turned around. The White Hen's entrance was clearly visible. Her eyes fastened on the door.

She knew that Kurt was more likely to use the door that exited into his building's rear lobby. But would *she*? Might the blonde exit to the street? Perhaps she lived in a building nearby and the deli conversation had been nothing more than that.

Harmless as ham on rye, Wenonah thought. Unless you're Jewish. *A blonde!—how trite!*

Wenonah watched for what seemed a very long time. If the woman did not exit to the street, it might not mean anything other than the woman also lived in the building.

Maybe.

The woman's throaty voice had been on sexy overdrive. Wenonah knew a woman on the make when she heard one. In the old movies she loved, such women were called hussies. Wenonah chuckled. The woman was an old fashioned hussy. Immediate assessment. Today there were other names.

And Kurt? His voice was neutral, nothing unusual there. No real evidence of attraction. Was he merely being polite?

Wenonah looked at her watch. Ten minutes had gone by without any sight of the woman.

She quickly climbed the four flights to her top floor condominium, pausing to spy from the window of each landing as she went. For once she wasn't wishing for an elevator.

By the time she entered her unit, Wenonah had resigned herself that both Kurt and the hussy had exited the store through the high rise's rear lobby. It was an unsettling and provocative conclusion. And innocent, perhaps . . .

Wenonah tried to put the matter to rest. She went into the kitchen, popped a Stouffer's spaghetti dinner into the micro and sat down at her little table to read the paper.

Concentration wore thin. Nothing but politics and celebrities gone amuck. Her mind kept coming back to Kurt.

The shrill tone of the micro alerted her that her supper was ready. Wenonah sprang into action, moving not to the counter, but to the hall closet.

It took some doing to find it. Wenonah's unit was cluttered. She was the first to warn her guests of the fact, but it would have been even more cluttered had she not stuffed her closets floor to ceiling.

It lay there at the rear of the closet, under a mountain of linens and towels. Without repairing the damage her rooting had done, Wenonah hurried to the living room, the powerful telescope in her hands. It was the telescope André had bought and left behind, his only legacy.

The living room had a bay with three curved windows. Wenonah carefully set up the telescope in front of the window that faced the Lake View Park building.

It would be dark soon. The last time she had used it, Meg had been here. It was the night of Kurt's bachelor party that began in his condo and then moved on to some unknown destination. Meg and Wenonah had used the telescope to try to spy on the party. They hadn't seen much, but it had been such fun. After the party moved on, Wenonah and Meg spent the evening gossiping, laughing, drinking, and spying into other units across the way. They swore to remain the best of friends always and forever.

Wenonah put the thought aside and started counting floors. The Rockwell condo was on the twenty-sixth. She counted up to twenty-five, for the building had no thirteenth.

The angle from the fourth floor of a vintage building to the twenty-sixth floor of a high rise did not allow for much to be seen. Wenonah would be able to see someone only if he—or she—came close to the window. In a very short time dusk would necessitate lights that would be visible.

That is, if Kurt had gone to his condo. And if there were two people there, chances were good that at least one would pass near to the window—or pause to take in the view of the park and lake.

Wenonah retrieved her supper from the microwave, grabbed a coke, returned to the window and sat. She ate but tasted little.

As dusk fell, she became more and more disconcerted with herself. "Just what am I doing?" she asked herself aloud.

It suddenly seemed so bizarre, staring up through a telescope in order to check on the fidelity of a friend's husband. *I've become a G. D. twisted sort of Angela Lansbury.* She laughed to herself but still felt foolish.

Something else bothered Wenonah, too: the sudden realization that she rather enjoyed the notion that she might catch Kurt in adultery. Why? She *loved* Meg! She didn't wish heartache on her for a moment.

But Kurt was another story. Wenonah had never taken to him. What was it? There was something strangely impersonal about him. He was good looking, strikingly so. He was polite and friendly to her. Not the honeyed kind of friendliness that masks prejudice, either. And he seemed to love Meg—he had been relentless in his pursuit. But where was the warmth in his veins, the fire in his soul? Oh, he did have a preoccupation for baseball, but he was a man born to business.

Wenonah acknowledged to herself now that it was his business that had turned her off. When the non-profit Ravensfield had been taken over by Hospcore, he became part of the medical establishment that was turning vocations in health care into numbers, statistics, money. Business. How could Meg not see that? His position as Vice-President of Finances was predicated on streamlining the hospital into a mega-money-making operation. It was he who called in the team of Anderson and Mertz, a consulting firm of lawyers without conscience. Oh, he was just a cog in the nationwide healthcare machine moving in this direction. But at Ravensfield he was a Titan. It was big politics now, screw the patient, screw the family, screw the hospital worker—social workers especially.

In choosing a career path, Wenonah had thought about Social Work, but her grandmother had encouraged her to take up nursing: "As a nurse, you'll never be out of work, Win. People is always sick, always dyin'." She was glad she listened because Social Work as a field, as a profession, was effectively being eliminated. Ravensfield had moved from eight to two social workers for the 400-bed facility. A piss-poor joke. A social worker there no longer addressed the real concerns, fears, and frailties of the patient. Psychological or sociological evaluations were things of the past. The two remaining social workers were there only to process the patients: get them in, allow them a stay as short as possible—shorter!—and get them out, finding for those with no place to go, *some* place, no matter how terrible.

It was the same way throughout the city, Wenonah knew, throughout the country. Kurt was not a major player in it, but she couldn't forgive him for the part he did play. How had Meg been able to turn a blind eye? Had she not quit, her job would have been cut, too, most likely, Kurt or no Kurt. As it was, when she left, her position had not been filled.

And now they were teaching nurses at Ravensfield and elsewhere how to do much of what a social worker does, and they were giving the duties of nurses—nurses' aides even—to social workers in order to blur the lines of responsibility, puncture job esteem, hold the line on salaries, and eliminate positions.

Down-sizing.

But now even nurses were on the endangered list. Underschooled and underpaid "nursing associates" were replacing nurses everywhere—to the great saving of the hospitals and insurance companies—but to the detriment of the patient.

It was fully dark now. Two hours had passed, and no lights had come on in the Rockwell condo. Wenonah's gut belief was that Kurt had gone to the woman's apartment for dinner.

Kurt *was* having an affair.

What other possibility was there?

Wenonah's heart sank. Any mean pleasure she might have embraced dissipated at once. She wished she had never seen Kurt and the blonde. She didn't want to be reduced to some needling, nosy Jessica Fletcher type.

She didn't want to have to tell Meg.

SEVEN

O N THE THIRD MONDAY IN April, after having dropped Kurt at the station, Meg began her new job.

The weekend had gone by without incident, without dreams, and she felt re-energized. She loved the idea of making her own schedule—and that there would be time to work on the house. Much had already been done in two weeks.

Meg drove south on Hohman to the Hammond suburb of Munster, a community that was upscale in comparison with Meg's neighborhood. Upscale, but characterless. No doubt, she thought, this is where many of the old citizens moved in the 50s and 60s when the city began to slide.

It was here that Clara Ivey lived with her sixty-year-old daughter in a little ranch home. At ninety, Clara was recovering from a broken hip. She was a large woman with long braids wound about the top of her head. She had a predilection for sweets, her daughter said. Meg found her as lucid and informative as *Time Magazine*. And funny.

Meg spent more than an hour with Clara and her daughter, developing a program that would meet all her physical and psychological needs. She left feeling something that she hadn't felt at her hospital job in some time: helpful. Truly helpful.

She was feeling powerful again. "Good things will come of this," she whispered to herself as she walked to her car.

Meg went home, had a bite of breakfast, and went upstairs to the little bedroom she had fashioned into an office. Her only call of the day had been successfully completed, and now she meant to do the required paperwork. When she finished she would go to the library and follow through on Wenonah's advice.

Meg knew about the pitfalls of paperwork at the hospital, but that paled in contrast to the volume of reports and forms that had to be completed for one simple home care visit. And then there were the orders to be placed for a hospital bed, meals, physical therapy and the rest. She had to call Denise Clooney twice for clarifications. Never mind, she thought, I'll get the hang of it and things will go faster.

It was well after three o'clock before she finished. She made some soup for herself, then prepared to go to the library.

Hammond Public Library was a modern building situated in the shell of what once had been the most thriving section of downtown. Meg pulled into the parking lot. It was a functional building, winner of no architectural awards.

"I just moved to the city," Meg told the tall man at the counter.

"You'll want a library card."

"Well, yes, I guess I do, but I'd like to find something out about the city and perhaps my house."

"Your house?"

"Yes, you see, it's a 1910 building and I thought maybe I could dig something up on it."

"Oh, I think you'll want to see Miss Millicent for something like that."

"Miss Millicent?"

"She runs the Calumet Room, top of the stairs. I think she just went up. A little lady with wild hair and red glasses."

"Thank you." Meg turned away.

"Wait, Miss! You'll want your application."

"Oh, yeah, sure." Meg took the form and made for the stairs.

Meg found the woman just closing the door under the sign

that read Calumet Room. Except for errant wisps, a plastic rain cap held captive her thinning henna hair. No younger than eighty, Meg thought.

She introduced herself and stated her mission.

"My, my, my," the woman clucked. "Oh, yes, I suspect I can be of considerable help to you." She clucked again. "But the Calumet Room is closed today, my dear."

Meg's eyes had already read the posted sign that gave the hours as two to four on weekdays only. "I see."

"You thought you'd find something out today?"

"Well, yes, I did."

The woman's forehead crinkled in anticipation of helping someone use the resources in her care. Meg thought the woman was about to make an exception.

"It's so nice," the woman was saying "to see you young people coming into the old neighborhoods and taking an interest in our history. This was a wonderful town, I can tell you. What street did you say you live on?"

"I didn't.—Springfield Street. 33 Springfield Street."

"Springfield? The big white southern-looking one?"

Meg nodded. The woman's mind was quick.

"Greek Revival?"

"Yes."

"Oh, my dear, the old Reichart place."

"Reichart?"

"Oh, yes, A very powerful family at the turn of the century, I should say. Lawyers and later, relatives that were judges. Powerful folks. My church elders whispered about some tragedy that went on there, but I was too young to take notice. A bit of a mystery, that. They sold it eventually and it's changed hands several times in recent years. Oh, I'm sure you can resurrect some rich history, little anecdotes, you know. My dear, we'll have great fun going through it."

"Then you'll help me?"

"Of course, child! But not today." Miss Millicent looked at her watch. "Landsakes, it's getting late and I have a train to catch."

"Oh."

"Don't look so disappointed. We must put off our fun only for now—what did you say your name was?"

"Meg—Meg Rockwell."

"Rockwell? Not a Hammond name." The old woman winked behind her red-framed glasses. "Until now, my dear.—Now I must be off!"

Meg was mentally adjusting the time of her home care visit for the next day so she could get to the library by two. "I'll stop by tomorrow, then. Two o'clock sharp."

"Oh, goodness me, I won't be here."

"But the sign— "

"This is my vacation week, had to take it, you see. Only just stopped in for my umbrella on the way to the station. My sister in South Bend is ailing. Poor Bridget, eighty-five, you know. *Older* sister. Getting up there, wouldn't you say? I should be back next week, Mary. We'll get down to business then."

Meg was crushed. She would have to wait a full week. "Isn't there someone else who could give me access to the Calumet Room?"

The woman's eyes widened, her offense magnified by the thick lenses. "I should say not!" she declared. "The Calumet Room is in my sole care, has been since '55. The room will be locked until the day I return, young lady."

"I see." Was the woman a bit daft? She hadn't even gotten her name right.

"Ah, I can see you're anxious to find things out. What is it you're looking for?"

"I—I don't quite know."

"Then it can't be *that* important." The woman's hand patted Meg's. "Why, just think how much more interesting it will be after you've had to wait a bit."

Meg was still considering the little setback when she arrived home. There were things to be found out, she was certain. Secrets closed to her now for at least a week.

The red light on the answering machine was blinking.

"Hello, there," came the unusually serious voice. "I . . . I have something to tell you, Meg. Call me."

Meg was feeling suddenly too tired, too deflated to deal with anything else. Probably some politics at the hospital, and that was the last thing she wanted to hear about.

She went into the bedroom to lie down. Perhaps tomorrow she would return Wenonah's call.

EIGHT

A human being is a part of the whole called
by us "Universe"—a part limited in time and
space. He experiences himself, his thoughts and
feelings as something separated from the rest—a
kind of optical delusion of consciousness.

Albert Einstein

By Friday, Meg was fending off real panic.

The week had been hell. The intermittent tappings had come on Monday and Wednesday, the piano music on Tuesday and Thursday. At least, she mused, the spirit appreciated variety.

Spirit? What spirit? Whose? To what end was it making itself known? Meg had been too afraid to try to reciprocate contact. Wenonah had told her the tappings were likely signals, but a paralyzed Meg had been unable to bring herself to tap back.

And the dreams—the dreams were coming every night. The dreams belonged to someone else, had to! Why else the dated streets and clothing?

But what if these dreams somehow were harbingers of some danger to her? To her child? This seemed a real possibility.

Meg had become convinced that Wenonah was right: she had to tell Kurt.

Yet how does one tell her husband that the house they bought—a house he did not want initially, or perhaps at all—is a *haunted* house? It sounded to Meg like a premise for a Chevy Chase movie.

But there was nothing funny here. Bizarre, yes. And frightening. She had never in thirty-seven years given any real consideration to ghosts, or spirits, or poltergeists. Now, however, she knew with certainty there could be no other possibility: the house held a spirit.

Meg sat in the bay brooding. She did not look forward to picking Kurt up at the station. How would she tell him? Over dinner? After dinner? Before? Should she cook? Should they eat out? Where?

Her mind played out a dozen scenarios—all the way through to the telling of the story. Each scenario led to a kind of dead end, for she could not imagine Kurt's reaction.

She had no control over Kurt's reaction, she decided finally, so she worked only on her part—the telling.

Meg's attention was taken up by an old Buick that slowed down and stopped across the street. A woman in a dark coat got out of the car, her gaze fixed upon the house. Meg noticed now that the woman had a camera in her hand. In less than thirty seconds, the picture of the house was snapped and the woman was on her way.

This was not a wholly uncommon experience. White and architecturally significant, the house stood out on the block, like a castle on the heath. Meg had seen others taking pictures of it, as well. It had made her so proud, but she felt a bit less so now.

Her mind came back to the thought at hand and her heart raced. She settled on telling Kurt over comfort food at a new restaurant, a locally famous glorified hamburger joint in Highland, a town to the east of Hammond. It would be good to tell him in public. Kurt would be more likely to listen, she hoped, to respond less quickly, less emotionally. And if an embarrassing scene ensued—well, they need not go back to the restaurant.

The hardest part of the telling would be the beginning. Meg wondered how she should initiate the subject, sounding out several possibilities in her mind. *Kurt, what do you think of ghosts?* Or, *Did you know an unseen dividend came with the house?* Or, *I suppose I must look like I've seen a ghost.*

But it wasn't funny. None of it was. And she knew—if he believed her—Kurt would find none of it funny.

When Meg turned the Saturn into the station lot and heard the shrill whistle of the 6:20 and the clanging bells as the gates came down, she still had not decided on the approach.

She set her jaw and breathed deeply as she watched the train doors slide open, disgorging commuters.

Wenonah Smythe picked up the telephone.

She was exhausted. The flu was going around at work and she had been talked into working doubles through Thursday. It would be good money, she figured.

Each midnight she came home to find no return message from Meg Rockwell, and she admitted to herself she was relieved. It was such an easy thing to put off, telling your best friend to keep an eye on her husband while she goes about the business of bearing his child.

Men! Wenonah dialed the Indiana number. Her physical exhaustion weakened the mental defenses she had built and thoughts of André came back unbidden. Gone two years now. No word since. Not a Goddamn card. Five years washed away. *Screw him!*

She heard the phone ringing in Hammond.

They had been happy years, those years with André Dubay. A French citizen, he had studied in Chicago and interned at Ravensfield, where they had met. They had fallen in love, lived together the last three years of their relationship.

They had let nothing bother them; the interracial thing just didn't seem to matter. *Seem to*, Wenonah thought. She should have suspected something a year before the end, when he went back to France for two weeks without having asked her to go.

Although usually outspoken, she had not said anything. She just didn't want to upset the proverbial apple cart. How she had longed to go! But she wanted to be *asked*.

Then, three days before the trip, he told her he wished she were going—but by then it was too late, of course, too late for tickets, too late for a leave from the hospital, too late, she knew for the asking to be genuine. It was a manipulation.

Wenonah listened absently to the continuing ring at the other end. In hindsight, Wenonah came to believe that the trip was an exploratory mission to determine how she might be accepted by André's family. Or not accepted. She knew he didn't want to live in the United States, and on occasion they had talked of marriage—sometime in the future—and settling in France.

André was different when he got back. There was no more talk of their going to France. The writing was on the wall, but Wenonah chose not to read it until those ugly few weeks before he returned to France permanently. Without her.

Wenonah could not remember how long she had let the phone ring. Long enough to know Meg was not at home. Perhaps she had already gone to the station to pick up Kurt. Strange that the answering machine didn't pick up.

She hung up, happy for another reprieve and that she could go to bed without having been the harbinger of bad news. God knows, she thought, Meg has enough on her hands. Perhaps this was a sign she shouldn't say anything at all about what she had seen.

Kurt would be in Hammond for the weekend, she was certain. She would wait until next week before calling her again.

I wonder if she's told Kurt about the ghost.

70

Meg hadn't known what reaction to expect from Kurt, but she hadn't expected silence.

He sat staring at her, his face coloring slightly but his expression was inscrutable.

The waiter stopped at their table, eyed their unfinished hamburgers. "Everything all right? Is the food okay?"

"Yes, fine," Kurt mumbled. "We just got to talking. You can take mine away—Meg?"

"Yes, I'm finished, too."

"Coffee?"

"Yes," Kurt answered, looking to Meg.

"Decaf." She forced a smile.

The waiter left.

"You're angry," Meg said, once the table had been cleared.

"Why should I be angry?"

Meg threw down her napkin. "How should I know? Because I haven't told you before this. Because there is a—a disturbance in our house. Because you don't believe me. Because you think you've married a kook! Tell me, Kurt, damn it. Anything's better than your staring at me."

"Okay, okay." Kurt inhaled sharply. "To tell the truth, I don't know what to think. How should I feel about this? I don't know. C'mon Meg, give me a break. I just got off the train a half-hour ago. And then to— "

"You don't believe me."

"I didn't say that!"

"You haven't said you *do*."

"I . . . I believe you're sincere in your conviction that there is something askew— "

"Something askew!" Meg was interrupted by the waiter who brought the coffee. Her lips tightened until he made his retreat. "There's more than something askew," she hissed, once the waiter was out of earshot. "I've been nearly half crazy with this thing. I don't sleep—I— "

"All right, all right. Calm down. You know we don't have to keep it."

"The house?" Meg felt her lower lip quiver.

"Yeah, the house. It seems to be the source. Maybe it *is* haunted. And right now we have one house too many."

"Oh, Kurt— "

"Don't think I take it lightly, Meg. There's the move, the expense, your job situation— "

"It's more than that, Kurt." Meg tried to speak calmly, rationally. How could she make him understand? "It's more than a house. It's as if I've found the home I was meant to live in, to have our child in. I feel a part of it. I feel as if *I* had it built!"

"I get that. But what about what's good for the baby? And these dreams?—they don't sound too rewarding or welcoming to me. What about them, Meg? If they continue, can you live with them?"

Kurt had worked her into a corner. "I—I don't know." The child, of course, was more important than the house. Still she felt hot tears welling at her eyes at the thought of leaving the house.

Kurt looked concerned. "Enough for now," he said. "Let's see how the weekend goes."

Meg sniffled. "You're not angry?"

"Why should I be?"

"Because I saw the child's face in the coach house window before we bought the place."

"Don't be silly. I probably wouldn't have thought anything of it, either. Most likely, it wasn't anything at all, just some reflection on the dirty glass. Like you said Mrs. Shaw suggested."

The waiter came now with the check and Meg let the matter drop.

Kurt stood. "C'mon, my little kook."

Meg laughed and got to her feet. It was a ghost, she thought. It *was*.

―――――――∞○◯∞○◯――――――

Nothing unusual happened on the weekend. If Meg dreamt she didn't remember doing so. Still, she felt nervous and muddled. On the one hand, she wished for the music or tapping to occur, wished to prove herself to Kurt—and get his take on the phenomena; on the other, she prayed that such things were past, that life would take on normalcy. She longed only for the house and the child growing inside her—and for her husband's love and support.

Through the weekend, her mind was slow to make connections. She could not focus on any one task or conversation. Even the simplest of meals just didn't come together. An unexpected noise, or even Kurt's voice, would startle her.

Everything they were doing to put the house in order seemed hollow, purposeless—as if they would not be staying long enough to enjoy it.

They lay in bed Sunday evening, eyes to the ceiling. Kurt broke the long, awkward silence. "Meg, I think we need to refigure things."

It was one of those déjà vu moments. "You mean the house?"

"Yes."

She had prepared herself for this. "I won't."

"We have to, Meg. Look at yourself. You're a mess. A nervous wreck."

"I'm sorry. It might be the pregnancy, too. You know, the hormone factor."

"And you know it's more than that. Everything was fine before this move. This house disturbs you— "

"You don't believe me—about the noises, the music— "

"Look, if you say so, I believe. But the bottom line is that you're pregnant with our child and this house isn't doing you any good."

"Yes, it is. You don't have any idea. I love this house. I do, Kurt! Wenonah says most spirits are harmless, They just pull pranks now and then, doing things like running water in another part of the house or bursting light bulbs."

"Or tapping and playing music?"

"Yes."

"You mean you think you could get used to those things?"

"I don't know—maybe."

"Well, I can't. And you spoke to Wenonah about all this before you told me?"

"Yes. I was wrong not to tell you sooner. I'm sorry, Kurt."

Kurt reached over to take Meg's hand. She shuddered at the touch.

"You see," Kurt said, "you're afraid of your own shadow. You're afraid of me."

"I'm not afraid of you, Kurt. Don't be silly. What I'm afraid of is your saying we can't keep the house."

Kurt sighed. "Is the house more important than the baby?"

"No, of course not."

"You think you can have both."

"Yes. I want to try."

He let out a long sigh. "You're determined?"

"Yes."

"Tell you what, we'll give it two more weeks."

"What?" It was more a gasp than a word. Meg turned to look at Kurt.

"Two weeks to get my old Meg back. Two weeks before I personally post the For Sale sign in the front yard."

"A month!"

"Two weeks."

"Three, then."

"Okay, three. No more. Now, come here." Kurt slid his arm

around Meg's shoulders and pulled her to his side. "You're cold, let me warm you."

"That would be nice."

He whispered into her ear now: "Three weeks, Meg. That's all."

Later, Meg slept on her side, her back to Kurt.

It was a good sleep punctuated by the periodic pulling of the covers. She tried to cling to them, for the room was chilly. Even in her half-sleep she thought how she would chide him in the morning for being a covers hog.

When the alarm went off at six a.m., Meg found herself alone in bed, shivering with cold. She could hear Kurt shaving in the adjacent bathroom.

"Up already?" she called, feeling for the lost covers.

"Yeah, I was freezing to death," Kurt called back. "You weren't about to give your old man a corner of the blankets, you bad girl."

"You mean I took them from *you*?"

"Damn right! We had a tug of war in the middle of the night." Kurt stepped out from the bathroom, towel about his trim waist, shaver in hand, the left side of his face white with lather. "And then when I got up this morning I find all the covers on the floor at the foot of the bed. What's the deal?" He used the shaver to motion accusingly. He was smiling.

"I did that?"

"It wasn't me, honeybunch." Kurt retreated into the bathroom. Minutes passed.

Meg waited until she heard his shower running before she sat up on the side of the bed. She craned her neck to look over at the covers on the floor. In the dark, Kurt hadn't noticed, but Meg's heart stopped for a moment when she saw the covers there, not piled, but neatly folded.

It was not the cold of the room that took her now—it was an inner bone-piercing chill that violently shook her.

It came back to her, one of Wenonah's acquired bits of ghost trivia: one of their pranks, she said, was to tamper with a victim's bedclothes.

Meg listened absently as Kurt sang softly in the shower. She would say nothing to him, she decided.

Victim.—Is that what I am?

She tried to control her shaking, the rapidity of her heartbeat. The spirit, ghost, poltergeist—whatever the hell it was—had overstepped another boundary.

The boundary of touch.

NINE

The bar, close to Wrigley Field, was a familiar one, but Kurt felt stiff and uncomfortable.

The waitress placed two draft beers on the wood-grained formica table, smiled prettily at the regular customers, and disappeared into the late afternoon crowd.

"What are your hopes for the Cubs this year, Kurt?"

"Oh, I don't know. Haven't thought much about it."

"Yeah? Since when? Hey, you do have hopes? Last year's results didn't put you off?"

"Not likely. When has it ever? I've always got hope. That way we're left with *something* at the end of the season."

The two laughed. Raising his stein, Kurt surveyed George Ringbloom's long, handsome, honest face. He wondered if he was doing the right thing. Had he miscalculated? Hell, he needed to talk to someone. And who better that a psychiatrist? But maybe it shouldn't be a friend and coworker. Maybe it shouldn't be someone who knows Meg.

"Okay, Kurt, I get the sense that you didn't suggest a beer after work to divine a winning season for the Cubbies. What's up?"

Kurt flushed. He tried to laugh it off. "It hasn't worked yet, has it? The Cubs, I mean." He felt foolish now. "No, George, I . . . I— "

"How's Meg? How does she like Hammond?"

Kurt inwardly winced. God, psychiatrists are good at cutting to the chase.

"Problems of the marriage variety?"

"Not really." George Ringbloom had seen Kurt through an ugly divorce a decade previous. He knew Kurt well, and Kurt didn't want him to think his marriage to Meg was a rerun of the first failure. "The problem is rather—that is, extremely unusual. And, yes, it does concern Meg."

George finished a hearty gulp and set his glass down. The hazel eyes seemed rounder. "Now you take one, too. And then I'm all ears." He winked. "I won't even put you on the clock."

"Thanks!" Kurt laughed, lifting his glass. He knew there was no going back now. He took a long drink, then started his—Meg's—story: the face at the window, the tappings, the piano music, the dreams. Even as the story unfolded in his laconic manner, it didn't take as long as he'd imagined.

George listened without interruption, and his face had taken on a ponderous expression by the time the tale was told.

"Well— ?" Kurt pressed. "Meg thinks it's a ghost or poltergeist or some damn thing."

"And you?"

"Me?"

"Do *you* believe?"

"No. I mean, I don't know. Maybe if I had experienced even one of those things, it'd be different. But I haven't." He paused, drawing in breath. "George, can there—are there such things?"

"Ghosts? Well, this is hardly my field of expertise, Kurt. Unless you think it's all coming from *within* Meg."

Kurt felt traitorous and ashamed, yet he asked, "Is *that* possible?"

"Kurt, our minds are capable of some very powerful and strange things, but most of what you've described seems to be tied into this old house. You know, I'd love to see it."

"So there *are* hauntings."

"Some are harder to prove than others."

"George— "

"Do I believe?" George set down his glass and leveled his most professional gaze at Kurt. "Yes, absolutely."

Kurt felt the breath go out of him. He became strangely dizzy. Ghosts are possible, he thought. *My God, I own a Goddamn haunted house.*

Now he realized George was still speaking.

"—what's really interesting, Kurt, in fact, damn fascinating, is those dreams. Very unusual. And they seem almost a separate issue from those other phenomena."

"What do you mean?"

"Well, they reflect an inner sort of happening as opposed to occurrences that can be perceived by the senses."

"The music and tapping?"

"Yes."

"I see. And the dreams may be separate from the physical haunting, if that's what it is?"

George shrugged, hesitant to continue.

"There must be a connection, yes? Hey, dreams are in your realm, George, let's face it. You know my next question."

"What's causing them?"

Kurt nodded. "Exactly."

"I don't think dreams of this type are up my alley. If I thought Meg was subconsciously creating them— "

"You don't?"

"Not with the kinds of things in them you've mentioned— things out of a long ago past."

"Then where are they coming from?"

"Different experts will give you different theories."

"Like what?"

George carefully set down his empty glass, eyeing Kurt. "How much of a believer are you, Kurt?"

"In what?"

"The unseen, the unexperienced."

Kurt could feel the tightness of his own smile. "Not much of one, I suppose." He shifted in his seat. "Let's get back to the experts you're talking about."

George cleared his throat. "Some might cite reincarnation." He deliberately paused, checking Kurt's reaction.

"Oh, come on," Kurt laughed. "Meg said something about that, too. It's rubbish."

"Look, I'm just telling you what some avenues of investigation might be."

"You're playing devil's advocate? You don't seriously believe— "

"I've learned not to *not* believe, Kurt. It works well in my line. In any line, for that matter."

The waitress came and filled their glasses.

Kurt stared off into space for a moment then collected himself. "Okay, what's another possibility?"

"That it's a mystery none of us will crack."

"That's a cop-out."

George laughed. "Often it's the truth, but you're right, the experts would never get noticed or paid for their services if they were always truthful."

"So? That's it?"

"No." The keen hazel eyes held Kurt's. "Do you know what a hologram is, Kurt?"

"Yeah, sure. It's one of those things that has—well, it's like a photograph with dimensions to it. Meg gave me one of those Fossil watches with a train hologram. You turn it and it seems to be in motion."

George nodded. "There's this new theory—actually not new at all—it's just that it's caught the imagination of the New Age crowd. Anyway, it likens our very reality to that of a hologram. I'm not sure I can explain the makings of a hologram, but here goes: A hologram is achieved by splitting a laser light into two rays using a splitter. The first beam hits the item being photographed, say a table, while the second interferes with the light of the first as it is reflected off the item. The resulting photograph is a hologram."

"So how do we fit into the picture?"

"Well—and this is really cool stuff—according to one of Einstein's compatriots, a guy by the name of Bohm—I think—our individual realities are like a projected holographic image. The larger picture, the universe, is like the hologram itself."

Kurt struggled to digest the information.

"Look," George said, recognizing Kurt's confusion, "our immediate experience is one of three dimensions. No stretch there. But the holographic theory is that matter and consciousness are part of a whole. Within each of us, our beings, is a reflection of the whole."

"Oh, kind of like DNA? The Jurassic Park thing? With a tiny bit of DNA you could produce the whole?"

"Right, except that from us comes the whole damn *universe*. We are—in essence—microcosms of the universe. Each of us has, so it goes, the potential to access every aspect of the world beyond our mere senses. Our psyches are reservoirs of knowledge and experience that are literally boundless."

"Okay, okay. I'm trying to keep up. I think I see where you're going with this. So, these dreams—they very well could be someone else's?"

George smiled and nodded. "You got it, buddy."

"You're saying we all have access to one another's dreams, thoughts?"

"I suppose you could say that. It probably happens more than we think. We're all part of one collective unconscious."

"But Meg's dreams—they're out of some other time period. They belong to someone who must be dead, has to be."

"Ah, my friend," George said, smiling, "time plays no real role in this equation. The linear aspect of time is important only to us who live and experience in the here and now. In the collective unconscious, there is no time."

"No time? I don't get it."

"My fault, I'm sure. I don't often have to explain this stuff."

"But do *you* believe it, George?"

"It makes as much sense as anything else. Yes, I guess I do."

"Then these dreams can be like— "

"Transferences," George interposed.

"Transferences from one person to another, from one time frame to another?"

"It's not impossible, Kurt."

"I think I understand, but I just can't buy it."

"Listen, I've got a great friend downtown, a psychoanalyst. This is her area, not mine. She writes and lectures on the holotropic mind. She's become quite the darling of the New Age crowd here in Chicago." George took a pen from his jacket pocket. "It wouldn't hurt for you—and Meg—to see her."

Kurt gave a dismissive wave of his hand. "I don't think so. What we should do is sell the frickin' house. It's the *house*, George!" Kurt studied his friend. "Or—do you think it's Meg that's the channel for this stuff?"

George finished writing on a cocktail napkin. "Could be a combination of the two. Here, here's her name. I don't have the number, but she's on Michigan Avenue. You should look her up. This stuff is incredibly fascinating."

Kurt bristled. "Not if it's screwing up your life, George! Believe me, I'd rather be talking about the Cubbies." Kurt pushed the napkin into his inside suitcoat pocket.

That's all I need, he thought, to go home to Meg with the news she's to see a psychoanalyst.

TEN

MEG WAS DRIVING.

The car, a two-seater, jerked into motion and gyrated along the dusty city street. Its vibration and high, whining hum suggested a speed higher than that at which images of houses and storefronts on either side moved lazily by, as if she were on an old steamship.

Meg's gloved hands were fastened tightly to the steering wheel. Black fabric enveloped her arms to the wrists, where the sleeves—held with columns of cloth-covered buttons—disappeared into the openings of the black leather gloves.

The car passed some of the stately homes of the city founders. Some were massive rectangles of granite while others were intricate wonders of Victorian or Greek Revival architecture. Then came a business district of foundries, bottlers, printers, bakeries, groceries, and—into a downtown area now—department stores.

Oddly enough, it was daylight and yet Meg saw no movement on the streets or sidewalks. Not a living soul stirred. Not even a dog or cat.

Where was she going?

She had no idea, yet the sense of urgency and repressed panic was clutching at her heart, tightening her throat, drying out her mouth and lips. She attempted to accelerate further. She desperately needed to be somewhere.

Where?

Find someone.

Whom?

The car sped along at a higher speed now. Meg looked to the speedometer and blinked at what she saw. It read 18 mph.

Could that speed be correct?

Meg looked up at the road to find that a human form had suddenly appeared a hundred feet in front of her. Her heart leapt within her chest.

The fast approaching figure was that of a child.

Meg felt her foot moving, as if in slow motion, to the brake pedal. Gripping the wheel, she thrust her whole leg forward, horrified to realize it had no effect. The car would not slow and she was bearing down on a small figure in a blue cap.

The child's head lifted. Under the cap's bill, the eyes were adjusting, focusing. He looked into the cab of the car, into Meg's eyes, and comprehended at once his incontrovertible fate.

Meg opened her mouth to scream as the car struck—pitching slightly upon impact—and rolled right over the boy.

As Meg struggled to scream, to give voice to the horror she had just perpetrated, she came awake with a start, clammy and breathless.

She had dreamt every night. The dreams offered a variety of scenarios: a night at an old-time stage play, a game of lawn croquet, a formal picnic in a manicured park with men in suits and fully draped women carrying parasols. In each dream she felt the same sense of urgency, the same fears tightening her chest as with iron bands, the same premonition of imminent loss.

The loss of a child.

The house was warm, but Meg shivered violently now. She was chilled to the marrow.

She wiped cold perspiration from her brow.

She lay staring at the ceiling, asking herself the now familiar questions. What are these dreams? What do they mean?

Her heart raced. *Why is this happening to me?* She was convinced that these lucid dreams were not hers. How could they be? Within them she experienced a Hammond of old, a world completely alien from the city she knew. Are they warnings? Of what? *Is my child in danger?*

And lately, after waking from the dreams, as now—or even in just passing through a hallway or taking the stairs—she would detect the smell of rotting flowers. It was strong enough now to force her to the side of the bed. She needed to go about the business of the day. She needed to forget. Yet, more and more, she sensed that she was on a collision course with whatever force it was there in the house. The thought scared the hell out of her, made the tiny hairs at the nape of her neck tingle and rise. With each day that went by, each dream, she felt herself moving inexorably closer to *something*, to seeing, to confronting this—*entity* that possessed the house and commandeered her own dreams, substituting visions of terror.

Kurt was right in thinking they should cut their losses and move. The dreams—and the other phenomena—most certainly had come with the house. And she knew that the settings for the dreams were right there in Hammond, a Hammond of long ago. She should listen to Kurt, the practical one, and pack it in. There would be other houses.

But by the end of the week Meg had steeled herself despite her fears. She resolved not to be driven off by the unknown. Some part of the house still welcomed her, still cradled her in the warmest and most comforting way. When she sat in the bay, when she ascended the stairs to the first landing where the twelve-foot stained glass windows caught the western sun, when she stood at the French doors surveying the balcony and street below, feeling the breezes and even daring to incite the old vertigo—these were the moments that she felt complete peace, happiness, and at one with the house. These were the moments when she would risk everything—even her marriage—to keep the house.

Meg worked hard to clear her mind of the dark fears, tried to ready herself for what was to come.

In fact, she opened herself to it as if to a secret lover, as long as it didn't prove to be a demon lover. She dared the force to communicate, to make itself known, to materialize.

At least that way, she reasoned, it will be under my terms. Such was her logic in her strong moments.

But what would be the consequences should some figure actually appear to her as she turned a corner or entered a room? How would she react?

She trembled at the thought.

Thoughts of the baby gave her the strength to fight off the dark possibilities.

My baby. I will have my baby and the house. I will.

———————

"Any occurrences?" Kurt asked even before she had pulled out of the station lot.

"Occurrences?"

"You know exactly what I mean, Meg."

Each day, by phone, she had assured him that the house was quiet. Lying in person was more difficult. "No, Kurt. I told you."

"Any dreams?"

"None to speak of."

"What does that mean?"

"It means none." Meg braked at the light.

Kurt pressed the issue. "What about the dream in which you were holding on to a child's hand?"

"No, I haven't had that one for a while." This at least was the truth. The light changed and Meg accelerated. "Why do you ask?"

"Oh, nothing. Never mind."

At that moment a softball rolled out onto the street and a

young boy came chasing it. Meg panicked at once. Her dream of running down a young boy instantly replayed itself in her mind.

"Slow down," Kurt cautioned.

Meg slammed on the brakes and the car immediately screeched to a stop.

"Jesus Christ, Meg!"

"Sorry." She was aware of her own heart's racing.

"You nearly put us through the windshield. It's a wonder we're not sitting here with the airbags in our faces."

"I said I was sorry."

"You overreacted. You don't usually drive like that. Are you all right?"

"Yeah, sure." Kurt was right. There had been plenty of time to slow. And the boy, it seemed, had not even intended to go darting into the street. Meg had given him a good scare, nonetheless. He stood frozen in movement, huge eyes on the car.

Meg motioned him to retrieve the ball. He quickly did so and beat a hasty retreat.

Shaken, Meg accelerated now.

Later, Meg would think back to how the subject of her dreams had been aborted by the boy with his ball. She had had the distinct impression that Kurt had something to say about them. But what? And she dared not bring up the subject again, having lied so emphatically about not having had any dreams this past week.

Instead, she talked lightly about the estimates for the kitchen floor and the work being done at the north end of the upstairs balcony where considerable dry-rot necessitated the replacement of the balustrade and balusters. The more she pushed forward, Meg reasoned, in improving the house, in investing in the house, the more it would seem theirs and the likelihood of moving would lessen.

Meg had trouble sleeping. She had not encouraged any affection from Kurt, and he slept soundly beside her. How could she open herself up to physical intimacy when she had violated the intimacy of truth?

She felt guilty. No marriage could survive on lies. Wenonah was right about honesty. What was a marriage without it? Meg came to the conclusion that she would have to tell Kurt about the dreams before the weekend was over.

Yet, what would he do regarding the house? How could she tell him and not risk losing the house?

She turned her head to study his face, angelic in sleep. Had she done him wrong by marrying him? Deep down, she knew that she had never gotten over Pete Stoltmeyer, not really. Was it obsession, this unrequited love of twenty years ago? Would she ever be free of it, free to love Kurt as he deserved?

Had the child and the house become more important to her than Kurt? The question put her on edge.

Eventually, she slept, fitfully.

<hr />

It was not a sound, she thought, that brought her awake. It was a sense of—what? Movement? Or perhaps it wasn't a sense at all that set off an alarm within her. Perhaps it was just the *knowing*. She knew there was another—being—in the room. Her eyes tried to adjust to the dark, moving up to the ceiling in the far corner where there seemed to be the frayed outline of something gray against the black of the room. Meg could not trust her eyes or mind. What was it that hovered there?

At that moment, however, her attention was drawn to the open doorway and to a glimmer of light that had come and gone before her eyes could fasten on to it. Meg lifted her head, peering down the length of the bed, past the bathroom, past the short hallway, to the square hall where the stairway up began.

Forgetting for the moment the gray thing floating near the ceiling, she stared anxiously into the shadows.

A noise now! Her heart quickened.

She had mentally opened herself to the force within the house, encouraged it, hoping it could be persuaded to desist. Sometimes, Wenonah had told her, spirits need only to be asked to leave, sometimes all that's needed is a positive reassurance, a kind of validation of their untimely death, earthly angst, or a wrong done to them.

If this was indeed a spirit, what was it that stirred it?

Meg had visualized how she would console it, reassure it, and then—ask it to leave—making her case that life was for the living and that she, Kurt, and their child now owned the house. It was their turn to live in it. And it was time for the spirit to move on, to pass peacefully and fully over.

But now Meg held her thumping heart, regretting having opened herself to any such confrontation. She must have been out of her mind! What to do now? She thought she should wake Kurt. She was as frightened as she ever had been. Wenonah had warned her about the danger of being captive to fear and it was her friend's caution that stayed her hand. She would steel herself. All of these considerations came to her within in the flash of the moment.

The noise had been a light thud, and now there came light, ever-quickening steps. Meg held her breath, straining every muscle to hear, to see.

These were catlike steps, she suddenly realized, as a profile of Rex came into view, his white patches glowing against his gray and the night shadows.

Running, he propelled himself onto the staircase and disappeared.

Meg could hear the feline footfalls recede. She smiled to herself and sighed audibly at her fright and its release.

But before she could put her head again to the pillow, another figure caught her eye.

Quickly following Rex was what seemed a young child, a boy. He was dressed in white shirt and shorts, white shoes and socks. There was no clearly defined edge to him, merely a fuzziness of motion to the bone-white figure's outline as it moved against the foil of the coal-black hallway.

He ran—or rather moved—in a floating-like motion and although he was slower than Rex—or was her mind recording it in slow motion?—his movement was more graceful, completely soundless.

He made for the steps, his arms outstretched in pursuit of Meg's cat.

ELEVEN

THE VISION TOOK ONLY A few seconds. Meg stared in disbelief now at the black void. Beads of cold sweat were breaking out on her forehead. She strained, listening for further sounds, sounds that might validate what she had seen.

Nothing.

Had she only imagined it? She put aside the thought of waking Kurt.

She felt for a moment now her mind pulling away, moving upward, away from her own body. She looked down, as if from the ceiling and saw herself pulling back the covers, sitting on the side of the bed, pulling on her slippers.

The surrealistic moment passed and the next she knew she was on the stairs, one hand clutching at the neck of her pale blue negligee, the other gripping the wall railing. She had taken no time for a robe. At the landing, under the twelve-foot high stained glass triptych, she paused to negotiate her turn, her hand guided by the cap on the newel post, for the moonless night allowed for not a glimmer of light. Here, she could detect the distinctly dry smell of ashes, at once acrid and sickly sweet.

Meg continued the climb. At the top of the stairs, she stopped and listened, mute as the little seated stone angel she had placed on the top stair.

Moments passed. Silence.

Suddenly she sensed movement coming at her from below at an accelerating rate. Somehow she knew at once it wasn't Kurt. Her heart thundered in her chest. Turning about and looking down into the stairway, as if into an abyss, she saw, against the pitch black, the gray form that had been hovering in the bedroom. It was moving so fast in its ascent that there was no time to call out or even step aside. She drew in a breath that she thought might be her last as she prepared for the collision.

At that moment the gray mass reached her and moved through her as if she were the incorporeal being, passing through her in a rush of wind and as if it were culled from the North wind, for it chilled every part of her.

So—there were two—what? Entities? Beings? Ghosts?

She stood there shaking from fear and from cold. When she looked into the dark upstairs landing, the thing had vanished. Or had it dissipated? She drew breath and nearly gagged on the stink of violets, rotting violets and what she thought must be the smell of death, the smell of evil.

The next day she would wonder why she hadn't turned tail at once, why she proceeded to move through the second floor, checking two of the three bedrooms and the two baths. But she knew the answer: Rex. They had been loving companions long before Kurt entered her life. She had to find him.

Where is he? she wondered, holding back panic. She intuitively knew he was in danger—but where? Even if the child she had seen—glowing white and moving in a strangely fluid motion—were a phantasm, Rex had been real. That fact she did not doubt. And he had climbed those steps as if the devil were behind him.

She came to the doors of the master bedroom. Opening them, she saw that it, too, was empty. But the smell of ash was here, stronger than in the stairway. She was getting closer to finding the child and, hopefully, Rex.

The French doors, always secured at night by bolts at both top and bottom, stood open. Meg's heart caught. The screen doors were open, as well.

Without thinking, Meg moved toward them.

As she stepped up and out onto the balcony, she looked both left and right. As she did so, the cloud cover conveniently shifted, allowing the moon to shed needed light, light that made the whiteness of the house glimmer eerily. From the weeping willow tree in the front yard came the hoot of an owl. Meg took stock. The balcony facing the street, the long section of the wrap-around configuration, stood empty.

As she moved to the left, toward the corner and the side section of the balcony that overlooked the driveway, her hand holding to every column as she moved, Meg heard the shriek of Rex's terrified cry.

She turned the corner to see Rex huddled at the far end of the balcony where the rotting balustrade had been removed in preparation for the new. His back was humped high and his gray and white hair stood on end. His mouth opened in an angry hiss. His teeth flashed.

The feline bravado, however, could not mask his deep fear and panic.

Leaning toward him, arm outstretched in a gentle, pulsating motion was the figure of the boy in white, glowing whiter than the house itself. The air was thick with the pungently bitter scent of ashes. He was reaching out to Rex, who had backed himself to less than an inch from the unprotected edge of the balcony.

The cat was cornered by the boy. It had nowhere to go. Perched on this precipice, he cried out now in utter terror, his head turning about and taking a quick assessment of the drop to the ground.

It was a distance he had never attempted.

Meg had observed Rex calculate his leaps and jumps hundreds of times, and they had almost always been executed beautifully—but now, from this height she was certain he would not survive.

This thought came in a split second and with such certainty

that she rushed toward her cat, her faithful companion of eight years, without a concern for her old vertigo. She prayed only that her quick action would not further alarm him, causing him to jump.

She moved like quicksilver to the end of the balcony. The boy's face turned toward her in a kind of astonishment. His mouth, so red against the paleness of his face, shimmered into what seemed a smile. She sensed immediately the boy had meant no harm to the cat.

Rex held his ground. By the time Meg reached him, bending and scooping up into her arms his rigid, trembling form, the white luminescent form of the boy had vanished.

Just as Meg stood and turned, looking for the child, clutching Rex, still terrified herself, she heard the cracking sound of the dry-rotted planks beneath her giving way.

Sensing the danger, too, Rex pressed his little back feet into Meg's chest for propulsion and leaped from her. While he landed on a safe and solid area of the porch, the planks beneath Meg's feet were groaning and giving way.

Rex's jump had upset her equilibrium. Meg faltered—and looked down.

In just a fleeting moment, it all made sense. It was as if a truth were revealed. Her vertigo, the childhood nightmares of falling, the sheer helplessness, the despair, the weightless stomach had all presaged this—the fall that would take her and her unborn baby to their deaths.

She cried out.

Or had she only thought that she had cried out?

The floor gave way. She felt herself plunging toward the ground in a sensation that seemed to last forever.

Down she fell, not as if she were falling from a second floor, but as if it were from a skyscraper. She was living the old nightmare.

Falling—falling—until—

The sensation stopped abruptly. Inexplicably, she felt cushioned now, not crushed but cradled by something, someone. Who?

She felt safe. Who had caught her, broken her fall?

She felt as though she were being lifted. She longed to open her eyes, but couldn't. It was if tiny weights were holding down her eyelids. And if she were to open her eyes, she thought, the danger and the terrible feeling of dropping off the edge of the world would return.

The upward motion continued. She could detect once again the sickeningly sweet smell of decaying violets nearby. Then there was nothing.

It seemed a long time before consciousness returned. When she opened her eyes, she felt stationary. Kurt was kneeling at her side, staring down at her.

"You caught me? . . . How?"

"No, I didn't catch you, Meg. You must have fainted right here. Damn lucky you are. You're so close to the edge that I nearly had a heart attack."

Meg saw that she was, indeed, still on the balcony, less than a foot from the edge. "I'm confused. You didn't catch me? I didn't fall from the balcony?"

"No, Thank God! Do you feel all right? We should get you to ER."

"No. I think I'm all right."

"Well, we'll get you to a doctor in the morning. Meg, what the hell were you doing out here?"

"What?" She paused, carefully choosing her words. "Oh, I heard Rex crying. He was out here. He was terrified. Kurt, you know he's a house cat."

"How'd he get out? The doors were closed and bolted. I checked them before I went to bed."

"I . . . I don't know."

"Never mind. Let's get you inside and down to bed. Grab me around the neck. I'm going to lift."

The warmth of Kurt's body through his light flannel robe felt good. He carried her into the house, and as they descended the long staircase and came to the landing between floors, Meg saw Rex sitting on the small lion's head table under the stained glass triptych. His huge amber eyes stared at her with an intensity and cognition that assured her that what she had seen, he had seen. What she had experienced had been real.

For the time being, it was their secret, hers and Rex's.

"Doctor, first thing tomorrow," Kurt said as he placed her on the bed.

"We'll see. I think I'll be fine."

"No, none of this 'we'll see' business! You took a fall, no matter how slight. Need I remind you that you have more than yourself to worry about?"

How could she argue with that? She looked into the blue of his eyes and was touched by the concern she found there. "No, you don't. I'll go."

"Good." Kurt nuzzled her neck for a few moments, mumbling something.

"What did you say?"

"I said you smell funny."

"Funny how?"

"Yeah, like dead flowers—or something."

TWELVE

Doctor Michael Horan pronounced Meg a healthy specimen. He cautioned her to take it easy and eliminate all midnight balcony excursions.

Meg had gotten the doctor referral from Lucille at Ravensfield Hospital, a fellow social worker and former Northwest Indiana resident. The doctor's office was located in Merrillville, a booming community several miles south of Hammond and a bit east.

Kurt had wanted to go, but Meg insisted he go ahead and start organizing the basement, a task previously scheduled for the weekend.

The visit to the doctor proved a waste of time, but the ride home afforded Meg the opportunity to think. She was glad to be alone.

She had fallen from the balcony, she really had! Yet, when she opened her eyes, there was Kurt saying she had merely passed out *on* the balcony. She had heard the cracking of the rotten wood beneath her, felt herself falling back, not forward. She was falling, losing herself into the dead night, the dead air—until—somehow—the rush to earth stopped and she felt herself supported by some ethereal force that held her.

How was this possible? Meg held tightly to the steering wheel so as to keep her whole body from shaking. A doubt surfaced—had she merely dreamt the fall?

No. Neither—she became convinced—had she dreamt the appearance of the little boy in white. Had the child spirit who seemed to wish only to play with Rex, who meant it no harm—saved her? And the baby. But how was that possible?

This thought that the child had saved her was countered when she recalled that the pungent stink of dead violets around her had overpowered the odor of ashes that she associated with the boy. It was the entity that had been in the bedroom and that had gone through her like a cold, ill wind on the stairs that had the smell of decaying flowers.

Meg drove on, oblivious to the surroundings, her thoughts on the boy in white. She was convinced it was he she had seen in the coach house window on that first day they had looked at the house. An exuberantly visceral feeling was building up inside her now, subtle at first, then strong and heady as she came to the only conclusion she thought possible: the child was a force for good, not evil. It was he, she was certain, that had saved her life.

And if he could not be persuaded to leave the house, to find his place on the other side, what then? How bad could it be? How could it hurt to have a spirit around that saves lives?

Her mind caught now and the exuberance dissipated. What of the gray being from the night before, the presence she realized now she had assumed was a woman. What had made her make that assumption? Was it the stench of dead flowers, the violets? Or had she in some other way sensed it—just *known* it? And why had Kurt smelled the dead flowers upon *her*? Had she been saved by the woman spirit?

Whatever the case, despondency set in. No good emanated from *that* presence.

The return trip to Hammond ended without Meg's having any conscious memory of the drive. Meg parked on the street.

The contractor, Robert McKnight, was very young but very confident, almost brash. He stood on the front sidewalk taking a close visual of the balcony when Meg joined him.

"So you think the whole balustrade needs replacing?"

"No, Ma'am, just the rear portion there on the driveway side. I got my man up there now. Your husband said you nearly took a tumble last night."

Meg flushed. Damn Kurt, she thought, I probably came off as a helpless, klutzy female. "It wasn't anything." And this ma'am business. First the doctor was younger than she, and now this kid carpenter with tousled brown hair and large eyes was calling her ma'am! She felt suddenly old. Just when did she get pushed across some generational demarcation?

"But there is one other thing," the contractor was saying, pointing to the dormer above the balcony. "See that board beneath the dormer on the right?"

Meg noticed for the first time that the horizontal board beneath the dormer's rounded roof was in disrepair, its paint blistered.

"That piece has to go."

Meg trusted him. "Okay, go ahead and replace it."

"Sure, just as soon— "

Both the contractor and Meg heard a cry come from the balcony at the north end, the area on the driveway side currently being repaired. It was an abbreviated cry, high-pitched—yet the cry of a man, a man in terror, a man falling.

"Oh, my God," McKnight cried, "It's Juan!"

The columned verandah on the first floor afforded Meg a clear line of vision. She could see now the man plunging to the hard-packed earth. But the height of the verandah's flooring—some two or three feet above the ground—spared her seeing the actual impact.

She winced at the dull, heavy thud.

There was only a sickening, dead silence in those few moments before she and McKnight reached the man on the ground.

Meg saw immediately that his leg was broken; it lay beneath him twisted as a pretzel. But he was alive just the same, dazed and groaning.

Kurt hurried out onto the verandah and looked down on the scene. His face was white. "Christ! I saw him hit from the basement window. I've got an ambulance on the way."

"Thanks," McKnight said, without looking up. He started to speak to the workman in Spanish.

Meg knelt down and held the man's hand. She felt helpless.

The phone rang inside and Kurt disappeared.

The workman opened his eyes. He still looked very frightened, very pale. He tried to move, but McKnight dissuaded him. His glazed eyes moved to Meg, and he made a valiant effort to smile.

As they waited, the man's eyes seemed to visibly clear, and he became very animated—and agitated. He pointed above, speaking so swiftly that Meg wondered if McKnight could keep up.

Kurt reappeared. "Wenonah's on the phone."

Meg shot Kurt a look of exasperation.

Kurt understood. He shrugged, saying, "I tried to tell her it wasn't a good time, but—well, you know Wenonah. Sometimes she doesn't hear."

"Okay, I'll come in."

Wenonah immediately regretted her pushiness with Kurt. She shouldn't have doubted him. It probably was a bad time to call.

Still, Meg had not returned her call. And she herself had found excuses not to call, not to tell her friend about the blonde in the White Hen.

She could hear Meg's footsteps now coming across the hardwood floor. Her resolve flagged.

"Hello, Wenonah."

"Hi, Meg. Listen, I'm sorry if this is a bad time to call— "

"That's okay. It's just that we've got an injured workman here. He fell off the balcony."

"Good God! Okay, I won't keep you—but—are things any better, Meg?"

"Uh, no, not really. There's the ambulance, Win."

Wenonah could hear the siren, too. "Worse?"

"I don't know. I took a little fall myself last night."

"Meg, you're all right?"

"Yeah, sure. Could've been bad—listen, Win, I've got to go."

"The baby— "

"He's fine."

"Good.—He?—have you had an ultrasound?"

"No. I just have a feeling it's a boy. Female intuition, I suppose. Listen Wenonah, I really will call you. Monday? And I want you to come out again."

"Sure, Meg. Absolutely."

Wenonah hung up. *Damn it, Meg, you think your life is complicated now?*

Juan was being lifted into the ambulance as Meg came out into the driveway. Even a fleeting view of his face told her he had been given a strong sedative.

"Don't worry," McKnight was saying to Kurt as Meg joined them. "I'm fully insured."

Meg sensed immediately she had missed out on something important. "Were you— " Meg started. "Were you able to understand him, how it happened?"

McKnight looked to Kurt, who looked troubled. Something significant *had* taken place.

"Well, that's a bit of a mystery, Mrs. Rockwell. Your husband says you don't have any children, that you're waiting for your first."

"That's true." Meg felt her throat tighten and go dry.

Robert McKnight shifted awkwardly. "Well, Juan said that someone tapped at the window off the balcony."

"That was enough to make him lose his footing?"

"That and the fact that it was a pale blond kid who—and here's where I don't trust my translation—who passed his hand through the pane—as if—"

Meg swallowed hard. "As if he were a ghost?"

McKnight shrugged in a kind of unwilling agreement. "I'm sure there's an explanation, Mrs. Rockwell. There was no kid in the house. The paramedic did say he likely had a concussion. The fall may have caused a hallucination or something."

"Perhaps," Meg said. She looked at Kurt.

He was not amused.

THIRTEEN

IT WAS EVENING. DINNER HAD been strained. The discussion about the house came afterward in the living room.

Kurt had stopped his pacing and stood now by the fireplace.

Meg sat on a wicker settee at the side of the bay. She fought back tears. "But you said three weeks, Kurt. You did! It's only been *one*."

"Three weeks of nothing happening, Meg. Enough has happened this week! And probably even more than you've told me—yes?"

"No."

"Meg!"

Damn it, Meg thought. She felt vulnerable, as if he could read her thoughts, detect any untruths. "Well, just the dreams— "

"The dreams that you said had stopped?"

Meg sat in guilty silence.

"They haven't, obviously."

She shook her head.

"Okay, well, the dreams may have some kind of explanation, but when it comes to accidents—two in twenty-four hours with real injuries and doctors and ambulances—that's when we draw the line in the sand. That could've been *you* they put in the ambulance today. Meg, you're pregnant and as such— "

"So you think it's the house? That it's haunted? This has convinced you?"

"I don't know. But if you do, that's enough for me to say *that's it, let's get the hell out of here!* Most women would be long gone. How can you still want to stay?"

Meg drew in a long breath. "I love the house, Kurt. Oh, I know it's been only a few weeks, but it's become my home. I feel a part of it. I know I keep saying that, but it's true." She paused, still fending off tears. "The thought of moving back to a city condo tears me apart. I don't think I can do it.—And I'm not *most women.*"

Kurt came and sat down next to her. "Sometimes we have to face facts." He took her hand. "This isn't working, Meg. But it isn't the end of the world. We can start looking for another house right away—here in Hammond, if you want."

"It's not Hammond, Kurt. It's the house. It's a once-in-a-lifetime house."

"Believe me, Meg, I do want you to be happy."

"Then let's wait. We may be able to get to the bottom of this—this mystery. We may be able to purge the house of whatever it is— "

"With what? Ghostbusters?" Kurt jumped up in anger. "At what cost, Meg?" He spun around to face her. "Yours? Mine? The baby's? Huh?" His eyes narrowed. "Our marriage?"

"No, of course not!" Meg paused, biting her lower lip and waiting for the tension to ease.

Kurt turned to stare out the front window. A minute or two passed.

"Kurt," Meg ventured, "what did you mean about there being an explanation for my dreams?"

The conversation took a sudden turn. Meg could see that it was he who felt suddenly vulnerable. His anger vanished. He had let something leak out. What was it? Meg thought back to the drive home from the station and how he had questioned her about the dreams, as if he had learned something—

"What is it, Kurt?"

"Well, truth is I mentioned your—occurrences and dreams to George Ringbloom and he brought up— "

"You did what?" Meg felt angry blood rushing to her face.

"I spoke to George about them."

"Without asking me? Great! So he and everyone at Ravensfield is having a field day at my expense! Poor Meg Rockwell, I can just hear it, Kurt. Poor Meg, did you hear how she went off the deep end? She's gone quite bonkers in Hammond with all kinds of imaginings—poltergeists and such."

"It's not like that, Meg! First of all, George was there for me every step of the way through my divorce and I can assure you that his confidence is as true as a priest's. Not a single detail got out then, and he won't betray my trust now."

Meg took a breath. Her anger was abating. She had to silently concur because had anything about Kurt's divorce gotten onto the hospital grapevine, she would have heard.

"Second," Kurt was saying, "I have to say that George lent more credibility and weight to your experiences than I had in telling him. Honest to God, Meg. I had to talk to someone about all this, and I couldn't bring myself to go to a stranger."

"Okay, okay," Meg said. "I just don't want to be known as Crazy Meg, you know? I do trust George. Now come back and sit down."

Kurt obeyed.

"Now, what did he say about the dreams?"

"Oh, I couldn't begin to explain it—something about holograms. Life is like a hologram or some damned thing. I know that sounds bogus, but he thinks your dreams may belong to someone else."

"Really? I knew it! I did—how?"

"I don't remember exactly, but it made sense at the time, sort of. You should talk to him, Meg. No, better yet, you should talk to this doctor friend of his that specializes in this hologram stuff."

Meg's mind was moving quickly. "So it is possible?"

"He seems to think so, says the science is there."

"This doctor, who is he?"

"*She.* I've got her name and number, but they're at the condo. If you're coming back with me— "

"I'm not—not yet."

"Then I can call you on Monday with it."

"Yes, please do."

"Meg, she's a psychoanalyst."

Meg blinked in surprise, then digested the information. "All right. All right, maybe that's what I need at this point. Maybe she can help us solve this damn thing."

"Don't count on it, Meg."

"Hey, this isn't a trick to get me to a shrink?" The question was only half in jest.

Kurt laughed. "No, it's not. And a psychoanalyst is not a psychiatrist."

"I know, Kurt, a psychoanalyst. She's not an MD and doesn't dispense drugs, but she counsels patients using Freudian theory. So she's a shrink. Next question: can we afford her?"

"That's immaterial."

Meg laughed now. "An ironic, even Freudian, choice of words!"

Kurt smiled, then stiffened. He made a move, as if to take her hand in his, but he couldn't bring himself to make the contact. "Don't get your hopes up, Meg. The house goes on the market Monday."

"You could at least wait until after I've had a visit with the shrink."

"I think our course is set, Meg. Monday."

Kurt's clipped comment reminded Meg of Captain Vere's resigning Billy Budd to his fate, a literary allusion Kurt would not understand. "But you'll call Monday with her number?"

"I promise."

And he would, Meg knew; he was as unequivocally forthright as the captain in the novel *Billy Budd*.

Somehow, though, she sensed that Kurt regretted having told her about the hologram business.

———◦◦◦———

Long after Kurt had gone to sleep, Meg went out into the bay again, and settled into the rocker.

Well, she thought, why not give in? The stress was getting to her. Why not admit it? And Kurt was right: there was the baby to consider. At thirty-seven, Meg could not afford to take her first pregnancy lightly.

Why not move back to the condo and regroup until after the birth? The time there would be confined and boring—but unstressful. No ghosts there yet—maybe in a hundred years. That is, if high rises hold up as well as the finely crafted old houses.

Meg took stock of her situation. The tapping had stopped. The piano music recurred from time to time, more often in her dreams or half-dream states.

It just wasn't *that* terrible. Did it truly warrant giving up the house? If only she had denied—not the existence of spirits—but the access she had given. Kurt wanted to retreat only because of the spirits' effect on *her*. He himself was a skeptic, an unbeliever. He didn't talk much about religion, for that matter. A lapsed Catholic, he didn't accompany her to Mass the two or three times a month she attended.

Meg blamed herself. She had mentally invited communication with the spirits. That may have made the difference. Perhaps poor Juan lay in St. Margaret's because of *her*, because she encouraged them to materialize.

She suddenly stopped rocking, her mind stricken with a thought both terrible and logical: Coming so close in time and description to her own similar mishap, could it be that Juan's was no mere coincidence? Could it be that he was a victim by proxy? A proxy for her because she had escaped unscathed? The thought was chilling.

Could it be that they were dealing with a vengeful and malevolent ghost?

Meg shuddered at the thought, then let it go. She had never been one to think the worst, and she would not do so now. Not about this.

In any event, her notion that the spirit of the boy was a force for good was put in question. It was capricious at best, and at worst—what? One thing was certain: there were two entities, one of a child and one of a woman, and one or both of them had to be taken very seriously. She drew in breath and thought for a good, long time, deciding at last that she would keep this information from Kurt. Telling him would just add fuel to the fire.

A noise jolted her now from her thoughts, a noise there in the room.

Before she had time to react or even think, Rex jumped up into her lap, his meow more of a whine.

Meg sighed in relief. Enough is enough, she thought, petting him.

She turned to the window now to watch the night shadows outside and the gentle stir of the new leaves on the old willow in the front yard. Rex began to purr. Will I be here to see it through even one season? she asked herself. Everything about this house feels so right. *I want to stay!*

One has to have dreams, she thought. This wonderful old house had become one of hers. How could she shake herself free of it, live her life knowing she had given up?

She thought back to her first love, her true love. Pete had been a dream unrealized, one that colored the years after him. But she would not blame herself for his loss, as she had for many years. That had been his choice. Having a child had been a dream, too, one that now included Kurt—and the house. How quickly, she realized, having the child and the house had become one seamless dream. How to explain it?

She couldn't.

And neither would she give up the house.

Kurt was putting the house up for sale on Monday. Meg had no reason to doubt him. Meeting with the psychoanalyst offered some vague hope, but how soon could an appointment be had?

Never mind, she told herself. She would not sit idly by in the meantime. She would be no sacrificial Billy Budd. There was action that she could take on Monday.

FOURTEEN

ORTUNATELY, MEG'S HEALTH CARE CALLS had been scheduled for the morning. With time running out, she regretted having taken the job—even if it was part time. She performed the calls as efficiently as possible, trying to avoid any sign that she was less than enthusiastic.

Still, her spirits were up. She had called the library early in the morning. Yes, she was told, Miss Millicent would be returning to work today. She thought of leaving her name but didn't. She wasn't sure the woman would remember her by name. Miss Millicent struck her as too scattered, too eccentric.

The morning seemed interminably long. Four house calls and not any one close in distance to another. She finished by noon, though, and stopped home for a light lunch. She wasn't hungry but managed to force down a tuna on rye—without mayonnaise—and a bowl of tomato soup.

She ate quickly and headed for the library.

The first thing Meg noticed in the Calumet Room of the Hammond Public Library was the carved wooden sign on Miss Millicent's huge oak desk. She did have a last name: Reidy. Fitting, Meg thought, she was so damn thin.

Miss Millicent was approaching her now. Meg's eyes fixed on the thinning, curly hair that must have just been subjected to its latest henna home treatment. Bare scalp was more plentiful than the hair.

To Meg's surprise, the woman *did* remember her. All right, she thought, maybe not so scattered, but still five stars in the eccentric department.

Miss Millicent rubbed her hands together like an overanxious undertaker. Her fingers were quite crooked with arthritis, the nails magenta. "Well, well, where do you wish to start—is it Mary?"

Meg smiled. "No—it's Meg. Well, the house was built in 1910, so I'd like to work my way through Hammond history starting a few years before that."

"Excellent! Precisely what I thought, too, sweetie. Come over to this table. I'm all set up for you."

"You are?" Meg was impressed—and astonished to see that she was prepared, indeed. The long table was piled with loose papers, documents, pamphlets, pictures, and books. The sheer volume was daunting.

"Now, once you wade through this, I'll show you some microfiche materials. Do you know how to work a microfiche machine?"

"Yes, thanks so much, Miss Millicent."

"It's what I'm here for, my dear. Now remember to keep an eye out for the Reichart name. That's the family that built your home. Johann Reichart was the patriarch. Very reputable!"

Meg chuckled that the woman could remember a name from ninety years before, but not the name of someone she has just met. She sat down and began to sift through the voluminous information on Hammond, where—as one advertisement boasted—"all roads meet." Kurt would have a fine comment on that.

She sorted through many items from the early 1900s. In 1910, she learned, the population in Hammond was nearing 21,000, the first five and dime was established, and citywide gas service had begun.

She became more and more amazed at the prosperity of early

Hammond. Its present state was just a shadow of what it had once been. New factories, foundries, mills, theaters, stores both big and little, and banks were erected, year after year. Interesting as it all was—the history, fashions, inventions, human drama—Meg worked fast. She did find a number of references to the Reichart Law Agency, but almost two hours yielded nothing germane to the house or the Reichart family.

She copied anything remotely of interest.

She was paging through one of the last books when a picture caught her eye. It was a photograph of a very slick-looking street; moving down it was a hulking piece of machinery that seemed to be spraying it. Meg thought it some kind of an early street sweeper contraption that sprayed the streets with water. But a close look and the photograph caption clarified the matter: it was a machine that spread oil onto the streets. The caption identified the "street oiler" in the high driver's seat but gave no additional information.

Meg walked over to Miss Millicent's desk.

"Find something, my dear?"

"Something odd. Look at this picture." Meg placed in on the desk. "What is a street oiler?"

"Oh, yes," Miss Millicent said, looking down over the big red glasses, "that *is* very odd. It's a wagon-tank and sprinkler. On dry, dusty days they used to coat the city streets in oil—to keep the dust down, you see. Goodness! Seems a colossally stupid idea now, doesn't it? I'd rather deal with a little dust than have my shoes and hem coated in oil. And can you imagine sending children out to play? My! My!"

Meg walked back to her table. She stood, staring silently at the photograph, her heart quickening.

Miss Millicent called out in a stage mother's whisper: "I've got the microfiche materials ready—whenever you are."

"Thanks," Meg answered absently, not taking her eyes from the picture. This was at last a payoff. She recalled the first dream, remembering now how oil seemed to blanket the streets, how it clung to her shoes, stained the hem of her long dress.

Meg copied the picture. Here was definitive evidence that her dreams were not hers. How could she have known about such a bizarre practice? Today was the first she had ever heard of oiling the streets.

Buoyed by this success, Meg moved over to the microfiche machine.

Miss Millicent stood nearby. "I've got the newspapers here for you. Mostly *The Lake County Times*. It may be a tedious task, but I'm sure you'll find something."

"Now, *you* didn't know the Reicharts?" Meg asked.

"Personally? No. You see, they were Presbyterians. My people were Lutherans. One really kept to her own circles then, not like now. Why, did you notice in those other materials how even the banks encouraged separatism by catering to a particular community, calling themselves things like the Citizens German National Bank or the First Polish National Savings?" Her laugh was surprisingly full and throaty.

Meg laughed, too. "I did."

"Later on they dropped the ethnic part. Not good for business— or community, for that matter! To limit yourself like that."

Meg set to work again. She found it painstaking, mainly because the name of Reichart appeared so many times, usually in reference to the law business. Johann Reichart had established the firm and had taken junior partners. Meg found the only reference to his wife in his obituary of 1905. Her name was Florence. Jason Reichart, his son's name, began to appear frequently after that in relation to lawsuits and advertisements for the firm.

The 1907 story of a land purchase caught Meg's eye:

REICHART PURCHASES
OLD HAYLEY FARMSTEAD

The text detailed how Jason Reichart purchased the farm from the estate of John Hayley, and that he planned to break it into lots for those wishing to live "removed from the stresses of the city." It would be called the Homewood Addition, a name Meg remembered seeing on her own deed. Stresses of the city, Meg thought, everything changes, yet nothing does. She wondered at the notion that her area of town—not even a mile and a half from the city's core—could be considered "removed."

Meg was at last getting into the 1910 files when Miss Millicent cautioned her that the Calumet Room would be closing at 4 p.m. Meg looked at her watch: less than half an hour!

She would gladly have spent the day there, if she were allowed to do so.

Her expression was not lost on Miss Millicent. "I'll be back Wednesday, my dear," the woman said.

"Not till Wednesday?" Meg's disappointment sharpened.

"No, I have a librarian's seminar to attend tomorrow. Always something new to learn, you know."

"Could I perhaps bring these files down to one of the machines in the main library?"

Miss Millicent stared at Meg in horror and her tone had a bite to it. "Absolutely not!"

Meg regretted the suggestion, but before she could cushion what had been taken as an affront, Miss Millicent walked briskly away.

The woman was left of center, Meg thought, nothing new there. But Meg needed her help—she must be careful to keep the woman in her corner.

Meg took no time to brood, however, and moved at a still faster pace.

She didn't know what she was looking for—not really. Some clue to the people who first lived in the house. Scores of families had occupied the house after the Reicharts: the tax records and old telephone books had given up that information. What if the secret were hidden with one of them? The house, it seemed, had not welcomed any one family for more than just a few years, sometimes not even that. Meg had her suspicions why.

It was her intuition that led her to persist with the first family—along with that first recurring dream. In it Meg was dressed in heavy, tightly laced, old style clothing. The setting of the dreams, too, with the hard dirt streets, storefronts, medieval cars, and an occasional horse supported a Reichart theory. And, of course, the 1907 photograph of the street oiler. How many years could they have gone on oiling the streets? Surely they were unneeded once streets were paved with bricks.

Still, she had no clear evidence that her dreams were connected to the paranormal manifestations in the house. But she knew that they were. Intuition again. But strong.

The microfiche images were flying by so fast she almost missed it. She backed up a page. Sure enough, a short narrative and a picture of the house, her house on Springfield Street! The caption over the photograph read:

REICHART HOME FINISHED

The article of August 1, 1910, highly praised the architect for the building that sat squarely on three of the new Homewood Addition lots, citing as key features its architecture, mullioned windows, Tiffany stained glass, verandah, balconies, and interior use of woods. Jason P. Reichart, his wife Alicia, and their three young sons were to take possession by the end of the week.

Meg studied the picture. The house today was little changed. Beautiful in its design—a kind of grand simplicity. Well, maybe not so simple. Knowing she was seeing the very first picture of her house lifted her. But what took her breath away now had to do with where the photographer—no doubt long dead—had positioned himself. He had placed himself far enough away so that it became apparent that the land on either side and immediately behind the house was merely farmland. Rooftops of downtown buildings stood in the distant background.

What wonderful views the Reicharts must have had from the verandah and side windows, and even from the rear! Today, houses blocked those views.

Meg was certain, too, that the front balcony of the house afforded a completely unimpeded view of Indiana prairie. No South Hammond. No Munster.

Just one sweeping, splendid panorama.

Meg now experienced something very strange. Later, she would not remember if she actually closed her eyes or not, but her experience was intensely real, vivid yet blurred, like a Monet. She was standing on the balcony looking to the south, taking in the landscape of gently rolling prairies, farmland, trees, brush, flowers—even their scents—the sounds and flights of birds. It was a majestic sight. She reached out and touched the wooden balustrade, freshly painted. Her heart was flushed with pride: *This is my house*, she thought. *I am the first to live in it. I will spend all my days here.*

The sensation—vision—lasted less than a minute. Meg was pulled from this other world by Miss Millicent, who was giving her a ten-minute warning.

Probably saw me staring off into space, Meg thought. She's not the only one a bit eccentric.

Meg could not shake the feeling that she had left her own self, if only for a minute. The experience had been much like one of her dreams: for the moment she had been that first person to walk the balcony, the first to say, *This is mine!*

Meg copied the picture.

Almost immediately, she came across another photo of the house, taken for the October 20, 1910, issue of *The Lake County Times*.

A group of grim-faced women stood on the front porch as if confronting the enemy-photographer. The caption read:

PRESBYTERIAN LADIES MEET

No article, just a short blurb that stated Mrs. Jason Reichart was entertaining the Presbyterian Ladies Group in her home. Missionary work at home and abroad was their topic of conversation. No one in the picture was identified.

Rotten luck, Meg cursed, *Alicia Reichart is undoubtedly in this picture—but where! Which one?*

She eagerly, methodically, scanned the three rows of fifteen or sixteen properly dressed, rigidly posed, unsmiling women, wondering, *Which one?*

Her eye was drawn to a woman in the lower left-hand corner, a woman with dark hair neatly swept up and attractive features including what appeared to be a mole on her right cheek—unless this was a blemish on the photograph. She had a strong frame, it seemed, and any curves were well hidden beneath dark fabric.

This is Alicia Reichart, Meg thought, not quite knowing why at first, just knowing.

She studied the face more closely. Yes, this is she, she decided. The face, the very stance. Her face was not so much grim, as the others, as it was—what?—smug? Yes, a kind of smugness and pride radiated from her posture: straight and tall, forward thrust, with hands free at sides, as if they could go to her hips at a moment's notice should the photographer displease her. This was the woman who stood on the balcony and said, "This is mine!"

Miss Millicent came over. "Find something, dear?"

Meg showed her both pictures.

"Bravo, young lady!"

"Tell me, Miss Millicent, do you know any of these women? Can you tell me which is Alicia Reichart?"

"Oh, I suppose you think I am as old as they?" She picked up the copy.

Meg immediately thought she had offended the woman. "Oh, I didn't mean to imply— "

"It's all right," she said, studying the faces. "To you young people, old is old. What's a decade after sixty-five? Am I right?"

Meg felt herself blushing with embarrassment. "Forgive me. Of course, you couldn't be their age. All of these women must be— " Meg stopped abruptly, certain she had only compounded her faux pas.

"Dead?" The word came like the sting of a wasp.

Meg was speechless. Her cheeks pulsed hotly.

"Oh, that's all right," the woman clucked. "I'm eighty-two. I didn't come into the world for a few years after this was taken. So I'm not that far removed from the time, after all. I'm a Lutheran, my dear, and these are Presbyterian ladies, so it's doubtful I would be acquainted with any of them—although . . . "

Meg watched as the woman's face tightened, her eyes crinkling and narrowing behind the red rims as she focused on a particular face.

"What is it?" Meg asked.

The woman's eyes were trained like a laser on one tiny bit of the picture. She set the copy down and hurried to her desk, returning with a magnifying glass.

"Lord a' mercy!" she cried, as soon as she placed the glass over the youngest in the picture, a girl in white and no more that twelve years old. A gasp as heavy as if it were her last escaped. "It's Bernie Clinton, I do declare!"

"Who?"

"Bernadine Clinton, my babysitter! My, what a flood of memories this brings with it!"

"Oh." Meg could not share her enthusiasm. This hardly seemed to advance her research.

"Why, I'd almost forgotten she was a Presbie. That's what I called them then. Bernie lost her faith altogether as an adult."

"I see."

The woman leaned over, looking Meg squarely in the face. "Why, maybe she could be of some help to you."

"Surely, she's not still— " *Damn!*

"Alive? Last I heard she was! Although she's in a home in North Hammond. Can't vouch for what kind of shape she's in. I won't step inside one of those places if I can help it."

Meg's heart was racing. This was the big break of the day. To be able to talk to someone from that era, someone who knew Alicia Reichart . . . Then came second thoughts. She stared at the picture, not fully convinced. "If she was eleven or twelve when this was taken, that would make her— "

"As close to the centenary mark, my dear, as a flea on a dog— you're right!"

"Can you tell me where this home is, Miss Millicent?"

As Meg pulled into the drive, she kept her eyes averted from the coach house in front of her.

She was ebullient. She entered the main house through the side door, carrying the sheaf of library papers under her arm and the little scrap of paper with the Hammond Retirement Home address on it clutched in her hand as if it were currency. It was a very successful day. Her sleuthing was paying off.

The phone was ringing.

Probably Kurt or the damn real estate woman, greedy for another quick sale. No doubt her mouth salivated at the prospect of making money coming and going. As she had pulled into the driveway, she could not help but notice the For Sale sign that had been newly posted in her front lawn. But she refused to let that deflate her euphoria.

Meg picked up the phone on the fourth ring. Her initial greeting was tentative until she realized it was neither Kurt nor Mrs. Shaw.

Her voice brightened now. "Hello. Who is it? Oh, Wenonah! Yes, what is it? You sound a bit odd."

FIFTEEN

M EG SAT IN HER BLUE Saturn outside the Hammond Nursing Home, a labyrinthine structure on one level, sixties in design.

Yes, the woman had said on the phone, Bernadine Clinton was a resident. Visiting hours were from two to four in the afternoon and from six to eight in the evening. Could exceptions be made? Yes, sometimes morning visitors were allowed if arrangements were made in advance. Ten o'clock would be fine.

And now she sat. She had not slept well. Wenonah's call had unnerved her.

She pushed herself out of the car now, resolved not to think about it. She would stay focused on this visit. After all, the woman she was about to meet had been one of the first to be entertained in the Reichart house—over 90 years ago. This woman as a girl had met Alicia Reichart, the first resident of the house.

The thought sent a shiver through Meg. She tried to collect herself.

Bernadine Clinton was a link to the past. Might she provide answers to the events at the house—and even answers to Meg's dreams?

The strong deodorizing vapors hit her at the door. Oh, Meg knew what Millicent Reidy had meant about nursing homes. She hated them, too. As a social worker, she had seen some terrible,

God-forsaken places, but even the good ones—the best ones—were depressing. She always mentally rated them like hotels: from five stars to none. She had yet to find a five-star.

They were places where people came to wait for the end of their earthly lives, many mindlessly, many drugged into a stupor. Maybe they were the lucky ones.

But what was on the other side? Not knowing was surely what kept many people holding on to life. Such was Hamlet's dilemma. Her mind pared a few lines from a soliloquy she had once memorized in high school. *But that the dread of something after death—The undiscover'd country, from whose bourn no traveler returns—puzzles the will, and makes us rather bear those ills we have than fly to others that we know not of?*

Meg felt lucky. Both her parents were still alive and active in their seventies. No major illnesses—yet. She knew, however, as an only child she might one day be faced with the nursing home conundrum. She prayed not. Not even a five-star for them if she could help it.

Her hand instinctively went to her belly as she moved down the hall to the front desk. Her own child—would he one day have to make a decision concerning *her* fate? She chided herself for the ridiculous thought.

Yet, how quickly the years did go! She observed the seniors moving along, or being transported in wheelchairs, their faces reflective of various degrees of alertness. A few were even quite animated. It was not that many years ago that they stood on the thresholds of their dreams. How had life played out for them? Had any of them achieved their dreams? Perhaps.

And yet—whether they had failed or succeeded, they were *here*.

Yes, Meg was told by a stout woman at the desk, she could see Bernie Clinton now; she had already had her full bath. Room 120.

"How is she?" Meg asked.

"Oh, she's a character. Lucid and lively—although she might be a bit blue today. Lost her roommate yesterday."

Meg didn't question it. In hospitals you often lose your roommates when they go home. Not here.

Bath, Meg thought, as she moved along an obstacle course bustling with morning activity and crammed with wheel chairs—many occupied—walkers, and carts. The woman had said *bath* as if it had been a daily ritual. Meg knew if a ninety-some woman got a full bath once a week, it was a luxury.

The place was as noisy as a psych ward. The nurses and aides, eager to get their morning duties done, barked out directions. Many of the residents were hard of hearing or senile and therefore they were loud, confused, demanding, whining. A virtual din. No wonder morning visitors were not encouraged.

Meg heard now a woman's blood-chilling scream. She looked up to see a woman in a wheelchair whiz across the intersection of halls ahead, mouth open, volume maximum.

She was out of sight and quiet for a few seconds, then as Meg neared the intersection, the woman rolled across again, screaming an encore.

Meg paused for a moment. No one paid the slightest attention to her, it seemed. Meg continued on, and when she came to the intersecting hall, the woman was gone.

To recuperate, Meg guessed, and to get ready for an afternoon performance. The thought was Meg's flair for black comedy coming to light if just for the moment, then guiltily put away. She continued down the hall.

Room 120. The door was open. The bed parallel to the hall was empty and stripped. If there was a waiting list, Meg thought, no doubt someone was even now being apprised of the vacancy.

The other bed was along the outer wall facing the street; a window near the foot of the bed allowed for some natural light.

The woman in the bed lay quietly, her eyes at half-mast.

Meg cautiously entered, stopping a few feet away. "Excuse me. Are you Bernadine Clinton?"

The woman's head turned now, the crinkled eyelids lifting to reveal startlingly blue eyes. "Yes," she said, clearing her throat and drawing herself up a bit. "I still am. Much to everyone's surprise." A smile played on thin lips beneath a birdlike nose. "Not going anywhere just yet."

Meg smiled. Feeling a little more at ease, she moved closer.

The woman was studying her. "They told me I was to have a visitor—put me in my best housecoat, but I— "

"You haven't a clue as to who I am."

"No, should I?"

"No."

"That's a great relief. I don't want to get like some of the others you'll find around her—crazy as loons."

"Really?"

"Trust me. And they're not just the residents, either!"

Meg laughed at the woman's joke. "I'm Meg Rockwell." She stepped forward and took the woman's slim, bony hand.

Meg wasn't good at guessing ages, especially when the subject was over seventy-five, but this woman's face did not look like it had weathered a hundred years. Her skin was quite good, practically free of wrinkles, and there was a vital sparkle of life in those blue eyes that made her—well, beautiful.

"I'm Bernadine Clinton, but I guess you know that."

"I do. Do you mind if I sit down?"

"Of course not, dear. I don't have any pressing appointments this morning. Just shove that contraption out of the way and draw up a chair."

Meg pushed the wheelchair to the foot of the bed and pulled a cushioned chair to the side of the bed.

"Thank you for receiving me, Mrs. Clinton." Meg knew how important manners were to women of a certain age. She went on to explain her connection with Miss Reidy and touched briefly on the research she was doing on the Springfield Street house.

Bernadine Clinton seemed pleased. "Just got a card from Millie a few days ago. Is her hair still as red as a fire engine?"

Meg couldn't help but laugh. "Yes, it is."

"Bless her heart, wonder it hasn't fallen out. She's a good one for sending cards. Doesn't come visit, though—oh, I won't fault her for that. You know she's not *that* many years behind me." She laughed. "She's probably afraid that if she did come we'd find a place for her." Her eyes shifted to the empty bed.

"You lost your roommate, Mrs. Clinton."

"Call me Bernadine, my dear. Yes, Elsie was one of the few sane ones, too. And young! Seventy-six. Stroke victim. Struggled here for two years, but just didn't have the will, you know."

"I see."

"Imagine, seventy-six. Come and gone. And here am I nearly a hundred. Can't trust the legs anymore, though. All swelled up." She shrugged. "I just wait."

Meg could see through to a vulnerable soul and instinctively reached for the old woman's hand, held it.

The woman's blue eyes flashed at Meg. "Oh, go on," she said drawing in a deep breath and withdrawing her hand. "Good to see a young person for a change, at least one that's not here to see about one bodily function or another—or are you?"

"No." Meg smiled. She had taken an immediate liking to this woman. "Do you have any children, Bernadine?"

"No, and that's a regret my husband and I had—but too late. And sometimes they kid me around here, you know, about the President, but I'm no relation to Bill, either, if that's crossed your mind."

Meg laughed. "No, it didn't."

"Not that he was such a bad fella." Bernadine Clinton fired off a variety of political opinions as Meg sat in amazement. This was a woman who read and kept current. She finished by commenting on a senator who had recently run for re-election in his late nineties. "Too old," she declared. "Too damn old!"

"Bernadine, I want to ask you something."

"What? Of course! I have been going on. Ask away! That's why you're here."

"I am hoping you can tell me a little about the Reichart family. As I said, I've purchased the Reichart house."

"Oh, the Reichart house! It was the talk of the town, I can tell you. A stunning home. First one on Springfield Street. It's still lovely, I imagine."

"It is, though it's seen some changes, some remodeling, over the years."

"It's had its share of tenants, too. No one ever seemed to stay long after—after the Reicharts. But to me it's still the Reichart home."

"You knew Alicia Reichart?"

"Goodness, yes."

From her purse, Meg withdrew the picture she had copied. "Here's the photo, Bernadine. You see, there you are in the pinafore, front and center."

Bernadine put on her glasses that had been lying on the bed near a Bible. Meg made a mental note to tell Miss Millicent that Bernadine evidently had found her faith again. Not an uncommon thing, Meg had learned, as people came closer and closer to the other side.

"Sakes alive, you're right! Why I can remember the day this was taken. Just like it was yesterday. I was praying the posing ordeal would be over with quickly. There was to be ice cream afterwards, you see."

Meg chuckled. "It looks like everyone was in the same frame of mind."

Bernadine laughed at the humorless faces. "True enough, but you see, picture taking was a serious thing. One dasn't smile."

"Can you tell me which one is Alicia Reichart?"

"Let me see. Yes, of course. Here she is, big as life."

Meg looked to where Bernadine's crooked finger pointed.

Alicia Reichart was the woman in the front on the left, the one with the mole on her cheek, the one who was attempting to hide smugness or a smile, or both.

The woman validated Meg's intuitive guess. She felt victorious. She was making progress.

"Did you know her well, Bernadine?"

"Well enough. She was a strong woman."

"I rather guessed so."

"I was always a bit afraid of her."

"How did you happen to know her? Through church?"

"Well, of course, there was the church connection. But I tended the twins on occasion to free up their nanny for an afternoon. But that was after the accident, you know."

"Accident?" Meg pulled her chair closer to the bed.

"Yes, they lost little Claude. Tragic, just tragic."

"Was he older or younger than the twins?"

"Oh, older. Claude was a year ahead of me in school. A real talented musician at nine. You probably read about him in your research."

"No, not yet. I've been working forward, year by year." Meg's mouth had gone dry. "Bernadine, what did Claude play?"

"Piano. Like he was born to it. Lordy! Like he was Chopin reincarnated. He was a prodigy, he was." Bernadine paused, as if to catch her breath. "Oh my, they had *grand* plans for him!"

"His parents?"

"Yes, but especially the missus—Alicia."

"He was that good?"

"It was eerie, he was so good. He was to go abroad to study and compose."

"At that age?"

"Oh, yes!"

Meg sat stunned. A child had died, one who had so much promise, so much talent. A child who played the piano.

Is Claude my ghost?

Later, Meg would wonder whether thinking about her dreams

induced one now or whether it came of its own accord, but she fell into a trance-like state that must have lasted two or three moments.

She could hear the piano music. She could see a little boy in white skillfully playing at an upright Steinway.

Beautiful, beautiful music. Mahler, she thought.

The piano sat under a trio of stained glass windows, windows familiar to Meg. The piano was in the former music room, the room that was now Kurt and Meg's bedroom. It was warm in the room, very warm. The chamber, relatively small, was crowded with chairs and well-dressed women. Meg, it seemed, was sitting there, too. People looked to her occasionally, nodding and smiling. The women fanned themselves, but no one seemed to mind the heat so engrossed were they in the music.

Meg found the experience oppressive. She was perspiring, growing faint. Others were lifting cool drinks with mint leaves to their mouths, but she had none.

Suddenly, something blessedly pulled her from the trance now.

A hand tightly gripped hers.

Meg's eyes focused on Bernadine and her heart tightened. Dear God, the woman's had a stroke!

Bernadine had pulled her head up from the pillow, closer to Meg and held on to her hand as if to a lifeline. She was pale and frightened. Her hand was cold, clammy.

"What is it?" Meg asked. Her free hand instinctively reached for the nurse's call button.

"I saw . . . sitting there . . . at the end of the bed. It was . . . it was— " Bernadine's eyes moved from the end of the bed to Meg, wordlessly imploring— "

"What was it, Bernadine?" Somehow, Meg thought she knew what the woman had seen. "Was it a boy—all in white?—Was it Claude Reichart?"

The blue eyes that had so sparkled were dim now. "No," she

gasped. "Not Claude." Her grip on Meg's hand grew tighter. Her mouth opened again, but the words found no way out.

Meg was in a panic. Where was the nurse? She thought she should run out into the hall to find one, but didn't want to have to pull free of the terrified woman.

Bernadine groaned. Meg was certain she was having a heart attack.

"Rest a moment, Bernadine. We're getting you help. Do you hear?"

Bernadine's nails dug painfully into Meg's hand. "A—Alicia," she said.

"You saw . . . " Meg started to say.

But there was no need. The head fell back, the hand loosened and slipped away.

It was another five minutes before a nurse's aide came in, chattering mindlessly about her busy day and wasn't it nice that Bernie had a visitor and my wasn't that the smell of dead flowers in the room but how funny that there weren't any flowers at all in the room.

The young woman was fully up to the bed before she realized Bernadine Clinton was dead.

SIXTEEN

I T WAS WEDNESDAY AND KURT hadn't spoken to Meg since she dropped him at the train station Monday Morning. He sat at his desk now, listening to the phone ring in Hammond.

Where the hell is she? The message machine came on and he hung up. He had left the shrink's information on it on Monday night. He had called several times Tuesday, but she didn't pick up or call back. By calling the house to access messages on the machine, he could tell that she had gotten them: they had been erased.

Until now, a day had not gone by without their speaking. He would try again later.

Kurt felt as though things were spinning out of control—as if he were losing control of his own life. He didn't like it.

His wife had become obsessed with this house—and now it was dawning on him that it might even be a threat to their marriage.

He was too practical to spend time regretting having bought the damn thing. How was he to have known? Or Meg? Or anyone?

Now is what mattered. Dump it—even at a loss—and move on without looking back. It was the proverbial white elephant.

———※———

On the third try of the day, about 1:30 p.m., Meg picked up.

"Meg?"

"Yes."

"My God, Meg, I've been worried! Why haven't you called back?"

"Sorry."

"Sorry?—But why—?"

"I've been busy, Kurt."

He was taken aback by her coolness. "This is crazy, honey. I'm your husband."

"Oh?"

"What's that supposed to mean?"

"Never mind. I've been upset."

"About putting the house on the market?"

"That's part of it."

"Mrs. Shaw called to say the For Sale sign disappeared overnight."

"Did it?"

"You know it did, Meg."

"I *didn't* know. It was there yesterday."

"And you didn't take it down?"

"No."

Kurt sighed in exasperation. He would get nowhere on this subject, he could tell. "Okay, listen, Meg, I know moving is upsetting you. Believe it or not, I like that place, too."

"Do you?"

"Yes, of course. But it's—it's not for us. You'll get past it, sweetheart. You'll rebound." He heard what sounded like a long sigh at the other end. "Meg?"

"A woman died yesterday, practically in my arms."

"What? Oh, my God, Meg!" He drew in breath. "Who?"

"Her name was Bernadine Clinton and she was a wonderful soul. She deserved a better end."

"I'm so sorry. It must have been a terrible experience."

"It was. And I'm to blame."

"You! This was one of your calls, right? And you just happened to be there. Shitty luck, that's all it was."

"No, she wasn't one of my calls."

"Well, who was she?"

Kurt listened silently as Meg told him about the research and the lead that took her to Bernadine Clinton.

"Well, it is terrible, Meg. But you couldn't have known. And the woman had to be old, yes?"

"Nearly a hundred."

"Jesus Christ!"

"But she was fine when I went into her room. She felt something—saw something. Just like Juan did. That was my fault, too."

"That's ridiculous! Now listen to me, Meg. I want you to pack some clothes, get in your car, and come into the city now."

"I wouldn't want to cramp your style."

"Huh?"

"I've got unfinished business here. I've started something, and I intend to finish it. There are two."

"Two?"

"Spirits. Ghosts.—Whatever! It's not just the boy; there's a woman, too." She spoke quickly and with precision, as if the words had the power to hurt him. It wasn't like Meg at all.

"Meg, please get out now. Today. You can't stay there alone."

There was a pause at the other end. He thought for a moment she was going to agree.

"You could take a day or two off," she said.

"God, no! I wish I could, but it would cost me my job. Seriously. You have no idea how intense it is here. You thought there was a money crunch when you left? You should see it now. I've been working overtime, sans pay, thank you, every night. There's unbelievable pressure for me to perform."

"You mean to cut."

"You got it."

"Was a time when hospitals were about people, sick people in need."

"I know that. But we can't always go back. Listen, I'll be out Friday as usual—unless you'll reconsider and— "

"No."

"Well, what are you going to do?"

"See that psychoanalyst for one thing. See where that goes."

"Do you think that's wise?" *Damn it to hell.* Kurt just wanted the house with its spirits to go away, just go away. And he felt somehow that George's friend would not be a step in that direction. If only he hadn't told her—

"I don't know what good she might do," Meg was saying. "I'll let you know afterward."

Kurt knew that tone: Meg would not be dissuaded from staying at the house. He glanced at his watch. He was already five minutes late for a board meeting.

"Listen, Meg, I've got to run. Big pow-wow. Listen to me, we're taking only what we need and moving back to Chicago this weekend."

Silence.

"Meg?"

"I heard you."

"That gives you two days. Be careful."

"I will."

"Okay. Good luck with the psychoanalyst. Really. Bye, Meg."

"Bye."

"Love you, Meg."

He listened now, but the wire had gone dead.

SEVENTEEN

Most people live—in a very restricted circle of their potential being. They make use of a very small portion of their possible consciousness, and of their soul's resources in general, much like a man who, out of his whole bodily organism, should get into the habit of using and moving only his little finger.

William James

M EG SAT ON THE SOUTH Shore train staring vacantly out the window. Clouds had come in late morning and still clung to the skyline, so she wore her light raincoat over one of the few dresses that still fit comfortably through the midriff. She would have to start buying maternity clothes soon, she knew, but doing so was not high on the priority list.

She was thinking about her conversation with Wenonah. The suspicion about Kurt that Wenonah raised—followed closely by the death of Bernadine Clinton—had left her numb. But now—with the train speeding toward her appointment with the psychoanalyst—she was forced her to examine her reactions.

How had things come to this? Did she still have a marriage? A real one?

Had Kurt been unfaithful? Is that why he was willing to stay in the city through the week? He had not commuted a single weeknight, something he would have been doing regularly had the condo sold. Oh, she knew the kind of hours he had been putting in over and above, but still . . .

She wondered again about his past, his first marriage. Why hadn't it worked? Had he been unfaithful then?

He certainly seemed to want this marriage to work. He had pursued her without allowing for the possibility of a refusal. Following their marriage, he had been attentive to her—even as recently as the weekends in Hammond. And he seemed excited about becoming a father.

But the temptations are out there, Meg thought. Wenonah had described Valerie Miller perfectly. Valerie owned the condo across the hall from Kurt's. She was a steamy blonde, all right, cool to other women, but with the opposite sex she was full of an Eartha Kitt verve and vibrato. As phony as a reality show. Had she seen Kurt's weeknight bacheloring as open season? Meg didn't put it past her for a moment.

And what about Kurt? Was he susceptible to a modern Calypso? Or to any other woman? What *are* his ethics?

Drops of rain were hitting the window now and beading into designs, but Meg hardly noticed. Truth was, she felt a sting of guilt for her own part. Guilt that she had not insisted he come out on some of the weekdays. She had to admit to herself that—except for those moments when the forces in the house held her in fear—she had absolutely relished those days alone in the house, and on weekends secretly looked forward to Mondays when she would drop Kurt at the station.

And there was that old, old sense of guilt, too, that in her heart she had never cleared away the remnants of Pete Stoltmeyer—and that Kurt couldn't compete with a memory. Intellectually she knew she had to put the past—and Pete—to rest. Intellectually she knew she could not compare someone in the present to what she remembered of someone two decades previous.

But, emotionally, well, she had not caught up yet.

Valerie Miller. So, what if it was true? Conceding—for the moment—that it was true and that Kurt had been behaving badly, had violated their marriage vows, could she forgive him? Would she?

When Wenonah had first told her, cautioning her that it was merely circumstantial evidence, she would have said no, she would not forgive him. But time had tempered her judgment—now she thought that she could put it in the past, had to, in fact, for she herself was guilty of a more subtle duplicity. . . . And the child would need a father.

Meg suddenly became aware of lightning outside and heavy rain whipping against the train's windows. She watched the drops as they struck, rolled, coalesced, and were wiped away by the wind.

She thought of Bernadine Clinton. *I have so much to answer for.* She was certain that Bernadine would be alive had it not been for her visit. Yet, how could she have known? Yes, Bernadine had said that she was just waiting, biding her time. And the woman sounded prepared, little knowing that Meg was her Angel of Death. Yet, those last moments—no matter how short—must have been ghastly.

Why had the spirit of Alicia Reichart materialized to literally scare Bernadine Clinton to death? At that moment?

Meg thought she knew—it was to prevent her from learning about the lives of the Reicharts. She had gone to see Bernadine for first-hand information about the Reicharts, and the woman must have had a wealth of it to give. But now she would be taking it to the grave.

Or most of it. What had she learned? Meg took stock. That Claude Reichart was a nine-year-old who played the piano with talent beyond his age and that his mother had great hopes for him. That an accident of some kind had cut Claude's career and life tragically short.

At the moment of Bernadine Clinton's death, however, more

questions were left unanswered: How did little Claude die? How did Alicia deal with the loss of her prodigy son? What was her life like afterward? What happened to the twins? Her husband Jason? What was Alicia's final fate?

Meg was convinced that it was no coincidence that Bernadine passed away when she did. It was part of a scheme. Alicia Reichart's scheme. She had heard of spirits attaching themselves to a person so that even if a haunted house was left behind, the haunting continued. Meg shivered. *My God*, she thought, *has this happened to me?*

She sensed—*knew*—that Bernadine Clinton's death was part of something implicitly evil. *And I, too, had a part in it.*

What was she to say to the Clinton family members at the funeral services on Monday?

The rain was letting up as Meg emerged from the Randolph Street station. She didn't bother to open her umbrella. The Michigan Avenue address was not far away.

She had been given the last appointment of the day, and at precisely 4 p.m., she was shown into Doctor Krista Peterhof's office.

The doctor came around her desk, shook hands with Meg, and introduced herself. Her Germanic accent was scarcely noticeable.

The two exchanged pleasantries and comments on the rain. The doctor then asked Meg to take a seat.

"No couch?" Meg asked, then immediately regretted the joke. She was nervous. She had never been in therapy, not that she considered this visit therapy. She was here for information.

"I have one there by the window, if you prefer."

"No, no. I wasn't serious. It's just the image one has."

The doctor smiled, sitting now in the winged back chair that matched the one Meg settled into.

Doctor Peterhof was in her fifties, Meg guessed, a bit plump but very agile. She wore a tailored gray suit and a white silk blouse, its rounded collar at the neck. Her silvered black hair was pulled back and wound into an amazing single braid that fell well below her waist. She smiled now and her Germanic features, not really pretty, gave the illusion of prettiness. She waited for Meg to speak.

"Now that I'm here, I don't know where to begin."

"It doesn't matter. Relax. What one thinks is the beginning often isn't the true place to begin. Isn't there some Dickens novel that begins with, 'I am born.'?"

"*Great Expectations*—no, wait—*David Copperfield*."

"Yes, that's right. Well, I'm certain Mr. Dickens thought that that was the very beginning, but it certainly was not."

Meg smiled tentatively. A bit of psycho babble, she thought. Still, the literary reference gave their exchange a leavening quality.

"It was a way for the character to get started," the doctor was saying. "A beginning."

Meg nodded. "Since I have only an hour of your time, I'd rather start with my marriage and bring you quickly forward to the house and dreams that I told about briefly on the phone."

"Good!" The doctor took up a notebook and positioned it in her lap. She took a silver pen from its holder on the desk.

And so Meg began. It took her half an hour to bring the story up to date. When she finished—with the details of Bernadine Clinton's death—she was fighting back tears.

The doctor looked up from her notes. Her face seemed to have softened. "You've been through quite a lot in a short timespan."

Meg nodded, thankful for the warmth in the doctor's hazel eyes.

"And you wish for me to shed some light?" the doctor asked.

"Yes, of course, if you can."

"I may be able to offer some logical reasons for some of what's been happening to you. It'll take some explaining. Of course, logic is relative to one's experience—and to an openness to believe. And to learn. You see, proof is often vague or nonexistent. And some of what you've described to me is difficult to explain."

Meg was anxious to get to specifics. "What I find most disturbing, besides Bernadine Clinton's death, are the dreams."

"The lucid dreams? Ah, now there I may actually have an explanation."

"Really?" Meg blinked in surprise. She had found the dreams the hardest to fathom. Even the materialization of Claude and Alicia seemed logical by comparison.

"Yes. But some of the other manifestations, I feel—like the tappings, the music, and the sightings—while they very well may be connected to concepts in my studies of the holotropic mind, they're really in a vague and mysterious area."

"The paranormal?"

"It would seem so."

"I see. Doctor, is it possible that I'm accessing someone else's dreams?"

The doctor smiled. "Absolutely—as well as their hopes and disappointments. "

Meg felt a quickening in her heart. "How?"

"Do you understand the concept of a hologram?"

"Well, on the most basic level, maybe." Meg laughed. "Don't assume too much with me when it comes to science."

"You're more into literature, I'll wager."

"Yes."

"I thought so. Now, I'll try to explain a hologram. A hologram is used as a good analogy to a relatively new science of the universe."

"So the universe may be seen as a hologram?"

"Exactly! To achieve a hologram, a photographer will split a laser light, arranging for the first beam to strike the item being photographed while the second interferes with the light of the first as it is reflected off the item. This makes for what you see as a hologram, a very clever image in dimensions.—Still with me, Meg?"

"Yes, I think so."

"Good! Now here is the analogy: each of our own realities is like a projected holographic image. Matter and consciousness are parts of a whole. You see, our bodies and our minds are parts of a whole. Within you, Meg, is a microcosm of the universe. You may not know how to consciously access the universe, but it is possible. Sometimes it's done with hypnosis or drugs, like LSD."

"And the reverse is true?"

"That other elements of the universe can access you?" The woman's pencil-thin eyebrows arched. "You are a quicker study than you let on. Yes, absolutely! Of course, some people are more sensitive, more receptive, than others."

"Like me?"

"Just a decade or two ago your dreams would have been described as mystical or mysterious or paranormal. But, now, Meg, the science of the holotropic mind provides answers."

"So, some force—or someone—can access me, and in a way kind of *possess* me?"

"There is such a thing as transpersonal consciousness, and it is infinite, but I must caution you—it's uncharted territory."

"Transpersonal consciousness? Then you're not writing off my dreams as coming from my vivid imagination?"

"They could be imagined, perhaps, but from what you've described, I find it unlikely."

"Might I be bringing these things upon myself? Like the governess in *The Turn of the Screw*? Are you familiar with that story?"

"Yes, I adore Henry James! And his brother William made a name for himself in science."

"Many critics believe that the ghosts in that story are conjured up as a result of the deep psychological needs of the governess."

"Could be Henry's brother gave him some ideas for that little masterpiece. I won't fully discount that idea, but your dreams of that house and Hammond seem to suggest the transpersonal.

Carl Jung's theory is that there is a personal unconscious unique to each person's experience and a collective unconscious that files away the experiences of everyone in one reservoir. Meg, you are part of the collective unconscious, but it is independent of you."

"And time?"

"Time doesn't matter a bit. Time is a linear thing that we grasp onto, but it doesn't exist in the holotropic mind. With the use of hypnosis or drugs, people have moved back in time—to their experience in the womb, and—if you can believe it, even before that—into previous generations."

"Seriously?"

The doctor nodded. "However, people who believe in reincarnation, people who remember parts of what they think are past lives may merely be accessing the transpersonal world, tapping into another's life in another era and another place—as if he or she—had been that person."

"So that would debunk the reincarnation theory?"

The doctor shrugged. "It would seem so."

"Okay, what about the specifics of my—my situation?"

"Ah, the occurrences. Like I said, Meg, this science, the world of the transpersonal, is new and uncharted. I may call it a science, but others may not be so generous. Some solicitously call it a theory. Some discount it altogether. Anyway, in your case, many variables exist. This woman—Alicia— ?"

"Reichart."

"Alicia Reichart. Did you bring the picture?"

"Yes." Meg took it from her purse. "It's just a copy—here, she's the one in the lower left."

The doctor took the picture, stared at it, appraising the figure Meg pointed out. "Yes, she was a very forceful personality. She just jumps right out at you, doesn't she? Her strong vibration is evident."

"Vibration?"

"Yes, each of us possesses a certain vibration, some individuals very positive, some very negative."

"I see."

"Yours, I would guess, is very positive. May I keep this picture for your file?"

Meg nodded. "I have another."

The doctor placed the picture on her desk, then sat drumming the fingers of both hands on her chair's armrests. "Let me say this first, Meg. I can assure you that I think you are a sane and rational person. I've no doubt of that. Don't let anyone tell you otherwise. And you are very, very sensitive—and that is what opened you to the transpersonal world."

"Then you do think that's what's going on with me?"

"This is what we know: the woman in the picture there was the original occupant of the house. She had a son with a very promising future—but who somehow died at the age of nine. How did he die?"

"I don't know. It was one of the things I wanted to ask Mrs. Clinton before— "

"All right. But death at that age is tragic, whatever the circumstances. This is the stuff of strong, strong feelings. Emotions, electric emotions that may cross the borders of time, may cross borders of people, so to say."

"And these emotions may have found a fixation in me?"

The doctor's eyes lifted, creasing her forehead. "Possibly. You said you felt an affinity to the house right away?"

"Oh, my God, yes! The first day. I had to have it. That is, except for the coach house. I have yet to go back in there. We plan to tear it down."

"Ah, the coach house, where you saw the young boy in the window?"

"Yes."

"Is the coach house as old as the house?"

"No, we were told there had been a barn there originally."

"On the very spot?" the doctor inquired.

"Yes, they used the same foundation for the coach house."

"And the boy's image you saw on that first day, was it— ?"

"The same as I encountered on the balcony? Yes, I think so."

"What scares you about the coach house?"

"I felt a cold there pass through me, and I just knew it was evil. I just knew."

"And the figure Mrs. Clinton said she saw?"

"Alicia."

"So it seems we have two forces."

"Yes."

"You've seen the boy, but you haven't seen a picture of him yet?"

"Correct."

"And we know what Alicia looks like. Mrs. Clinton did identify her?"

"Yes . . . then, they are, Claude and Alicia . . . spirits?"

"We're moving out of my area of expertise. I do know that some psychics differentiate between spirits and ghosts. Spirits have passed on to the other side, another dimension. On the other hand, ghosts seem to be unaware they have died."

"Unaware?"

"Yes, and as such, they appear to be more real than spirits that have ascended to a higher level after death."

"I've never heard that."

"You saw the real image of the boy. You were able to see him, perhaps, because he remains on this lower level, closer to our dimension. Whatever the case, you are dealing with forces, energy fields."

"Forces that are parts of the transpersonal world."

"Everything is a part of that world, Meg. Everything."

"Do these forces travel together, or is it just coincidence that mother and son—if that's what they are—are both suddenly making appearances? Is one aware of the other?"

"I can only make a conjecture, but in a sense the two forces may be one force."

"How is that?"

"In the study of the holotropic mind there is the notion of a *dual unity*. I say notion now; it's not an absolute. A dual unity is a very strong transpersonal connection between two people. It's the sense of two people becoming one, yet maintaining separate identities. Like a couple very much in love for fifty years."

"Or like twins?"

"Yes. An even better example would be a mother and child during pregnancy and the breastfeeding stage."

"But this is a nine-year-old child."

"True enough. But you have a mother who had great hopes for her son. To see them dashed, perhaps even witnessing his death, too, that trauma could have made manifest the keenest sense of duality."

Meg's head was swimming. "And so I'm left with two spirits— or with one force that might comprise a—dual entity?"

The doctor produced a nod that wasn't a nod and a shrug that wasn't quite a shrug.

No absolutes there, Meg thought. She tried to sort through her confusion. To what good purpose had this meeting accomplished? She glanced at her watch. "I think my time is up, Doctor Peterhof."

"I booked you last. That left it open-ended. First visits are always an uncertainty—not that you'll need another visit. Listen, why don't we go downstairs to the coffee shop for a bite. We can try to clear up loose ends while we eat. I'm famished."

"Well—I— "

"Can you take a later train?"

"I suppose so."

"Good! It's settled."

The outer office was empty. The secretary had gone home. Meg wrote out a check for the hour and the doctor closed up.

Conversation over their meal was polite and touched on topics as bland as the vegetable lasagna Meg was picking at. The doctor finished her roast pork special and ordered spumoni when the waitress brought coffee. Meg took a pass on dessert.

"We've been chatting away, Meg, but don't think I'm unaware that we haven't come back to your situation."

"Predicament is more like it." Meg put down her fork. "You know, I think I understand most of what you've told me—it's just that, well, I don't know that it's helped me."

"I hope that I've helped in two areas, Meg. First, in my listening and believing. Second, and this is related to that, I guess, is that I can vouch for your sanity."

Meg gave a little laugh. "Oh, I don't know. Not everyone would. I've been willingly staying in that house alone." Meg took a breath. "But what about the bad things that have happened—Juan's fall and Bernadine's death?"

"Ah, there is that. You feel guilt."

"Yes, of course."

"You shouldn't. You didn't ask for any of this. You just thought you were getting a house."

"Yes, not one with sprits or ghosts. Doctor, any idea which one I'm dealing with?"

"Spirits or ghosts? No, you might think about hiring a psychic."

"Really?"

"Really."

"You said there's a difference in the way they may appear, but is there a difference in behavior?"

"Oh, yes, the spirits are usually benign, even supportive."

"And ghosts?"

"They're to be feared and avoided, Meg. They can be quite malignant. Look Meg, I don't wish to scare you but what you've described to me are out of body experiences. OBEs, they call them.

It's also called astral projection, whereby the astral body leaves the physical body and moves to the astral plane. Some people have this occur to them at a near death experience or during illness."

"With me it was the house."

"And what may have come with that house." The doctor paused, then continued: "Some people deliberately practice astral projection."

"Sweet Jesus—why?"

The doctor shrugged. "Who can figure people, living or dead? Maybe it's the dare or the challenge, like surfers seeking out the most dangerous waves on earth."

The spumoni arrived for the doctor. Licking her lips, she took up a spoonful. "Delicious. Ah, it's good to be alive, I say." She looked at Meg now. "I'm thinking, Meg, that you want me to tell you what to do. Oh, you wouldn't stand for advice from a friend or husband—and you might not listen to my advice, either—but you're seeking it, nonetheless. Yes?"

Meg smiled. "I can see that you're very good at what you do, Doctor."

"Please, I asked you to call me Krista. Not because we're chums now—although I hope we are, this has been delightful—and not because I'm going to tell you what to do, because I'm not—at least in reference to staying at the house. You need to make that choice yourself. But I am going to caution you."

"Yes?" *Delightful?* Not a word Meg would use to describe their interview.

"Some say we all project in our dreams, and you may have unconsciously experienced these OBEs, but you've not been aware of them before moving into the house?"

"I have not."

"Then it is possible you are being deliberately drawn into the astral plane."

Meg's heart seemed to pause for several beats. "That's possible?"

"According to the people who have learned the art of

projection, yes. They claim that there are lower and higher levels on the astral plane. On the lower level, or dimension, the lost souls—or ghosts—and other dark entities are found. It's a kind of hell in which every imaginable evil lurks. They operate on low vibrations and feed on those souls who might wander in. Some experienced travelers claim that in weak and fearful moments they were literally dragged into this dimension."

Meg's heart was racing now. "How do they get away?"

"Those who have experienced such abductions say that they will it, that they deliberately call light or abundance or God into their life, and that they are released."

"Good God," Meg whispered. "And the higher dimension?"

"All good reports. Beings there thrive on high emotions, high vibration, goodness, and light."

Meg felt a shiver run up her back and her whole body followed suit and shook.

The doctor seemed to ignore the effect these things had on Meg. She continued: "Now, I want to tell you about a man in my field and the conclusion his life's work brought him to."

"All right."

"His name is Abraham Maslow. He came to believe that the psyche of man is not so terribly dark and forbidding—like, say O'Connor in *Heart of Darkness*. He believed that the psyche is the fountain from which creativity and self-actualization spring and flow. He wrote of the inner core of a person as having "impulse voices" that have to be heeded, that one should rebel against fear, weakness, and indecision. It is this inner voice that you must accept, Meg. It comes from your core. Accept it and embrace it. You'll then know what to do."

"Sort of like Dorothy in *The Wizard of Oz*?" Later, Meg would wonder what made her say such a thing. Had she meant it facetiously because of the strangeness of this interview and what she was expected to believe? Had she meant it at face value? Or was it a mix of the two?

Krista Peterhof laughed nonetheless. "Exactly! Listen to yourself. Isn't that what Dorothy learned? You see, literature and science *do* mix."

The next day, while eating a lunch of tomato soup and crackers, Meg sat in the first floor den absently watching some cable talk show she had never seen before. It wasn't long before the soup cooled and she was drawn into the program.

The host was speaking with an English woman who had recurring dreams and memories that placed her in Ireland a generation before—as a mother of a large family. The husband was alcoholic and abusive, and the parenting fell squarely on her shoulders alone. She was dying of cancer, however, and her greatest concern was for her children. She could not bear leaving them behind. Yet, she did die.

The Irish woman had died with the kind of strong, electrically charged emotions that Krista said take on a life of their own.

After years of these dreams, the English woman, in her twenties now, traveled to Ireland for the first time. She located the town that she knew so well only from somewhere within, then she found the very house in which the Irish mother had lived and died. Neighbors remembered the family. The English woman found out that her own birth preceded the mother's death by several years, so reincarnation seemed impossible.

The English woman went on to search out the children of the woman, who were older than she. Appearing on the show were some of these children who—while very skeptical at first—had confirmed details of the memories and dreams as perfectly descriptive of their mother's life. Further, they had come to believe that traits of the mother somehow resided in this woman that was younger than they. How strange! And, clearly, a bond now existed between the English woman and the Irish siblings.

The show emphasized merely the mystery and strangeness of the situation. There was no guest—no professional—to offer any kind of scientific hypothesis or logic to explain it. If only Dr. Krista Peterhof had been there, Meg thought, the theory of the holotropic mind and the concept of the transpersonal world would have offered the only logical solution to the mystery. And that woman's mind would have been eased after so many years of wondering. She had tapped into the emotional angst of that dying woman.

Meg realized now that her own mind had been eased—at least to the extent that she could understand the science of it. But she still had a growing curiosity and desire to discover the full truth about Alicia and Claude.

And—science or no—remaining in her heart was a well of fear over what she might find—and what they might do.

EIGHTEEN

M EG WAS WAITING OUTSIDE THE Calumet Room when Miss Millicent arrived.

"My, you are anxious to start today, child."

"Yes," Meg said. She could tell that beneath the cheerful greeting, the woman had been shaken by Bernadine Clinton's death. Meg had called her the evening before with the news. Of course, she said nothing to her—just as she had said nothing to the nursing staff—about the appearance of Alicia in the room.

The two women embraced. It was something that came naturally, and later Meg would not remember which of them had initiated it. Drawing back, she looked for some trace of suspicion or accusation in the lines of the old woman's face, but found none. Just grief for her friend's death and concern for Meg.

More guilt.

They talked briefly about Bernadine Clinton, then Miss Millicent went about her duties and Meg resumed her microfiche research. Her mind remained distracted, but she moved fast, nonetheless. Too fast, she worried—she might be missing something important.

Yet, she did make discoveries.

She found several articles detailing Claude's talent at the piano and appearances he had made. Mendelson and Debussy were cited as composers he admired. He often played their works, as well as some of his own. No pictures accompanied the articles.

And then—in the obituaries of July 17th, 1911, she found the death notice for little Claude. It yielded little, however: age, parents, visitation times at the Springfield Street home, church service and burial site.

Meg clipped through nearly a full decade in an hour, striking paydirt in a 1918 paper: a cluster of three Reichart obituaries within five days—those of Jason Reichart and his twin sons, Robert and Peter. The cause of the deaths was listed as "influenza," this at a time when the front page was carrying headlines proclaiming a citywide epidemic.

Meg shuddered. So, just seven years after losing Claude, Alicia lost the rest of her family in one blow. Her family had been decimated. What a burden it must have been! For a brief moment, the dark and unrelenting grief that had been Alicia Reichart's seemed to wash over and through Meg in galvanizing waves. In that moment, Meg didn't have to imagine the woman's pain and despair—she *felt* it.

She pushed on with her work.

She had just one hour's time left before the Calumet Room closed when Kurt walked in.

She looked up in surprise and her heart quickened a bit, mostly in pleasure. He *had* come!

His face seemed so very serious.

Meg smiled. "You did take a day off, Kurt. I'm glad."

"A few hours only, Meg, then I have to dash back. I borrowed a car."

"Oh—Okay," Meg said tentatively. Something serious had prompted him to drive out in a borrowed car.

Kurt looked around. A young man researching his family and Miss Millicent, who glanced up from her desk now, were the only others in the room. "I think we should talk outside," he said.

"All right." Truth was, Meg felt bad about losing precious research time.

They went downstairs and outside the double doors, stepping into the parking lot to stand face to face.

"I didn't come out by choice. Mrs. Shaw threatened to drop us unless she gets cooperation."

"Mrs. Shaw? Huh? What cooperation?"

"Yes, Meg. First, there's the matter of the For Sale sign, and then she said you were uncooperative and rude to her on the phone."

"No—well, I might have been. But she can be pushy and rude herself."

"She said you haven't answered the phone or responded to her messages."

Meg raised her right hand. "Guilty, your honor."

"This isn't funny. Meg, she's got someone interested in the house, and— "

"Who?" Meg became immediately on edge.

"That couple that tried to bid against us after we made our offer. We can't louse this up."

"What about the spirits? I mean ghosts?" She had no idea why this tactic was the first that came to her.

"What do you mean?"

"Do we tell them?"

"We don't even know— "

"Oh, yes we do. According to Krista— "

"You're on first name terms with the shrink? No! For God's sake, we don't tell them. We want to get rid of the house, Meg, without having to give the damn thing away!"

"So it's 'Buyer Beware'?"

"Exactly! I suspect that was the situation with us."

Meg glared at Kurt. "I'm not quite ready, Kurt. You know, I'm making real progress. I'm on my way to solving this—to putting the ghosts to rest."

"Listen to yourself, Meg! Good God!"

"They're troubled— "

"What do you think this is—*Hamlet*? I've read it, too, Meg, believe it or not. It's a *play*, with *medieval* notions about ghosts and why they can't rest."

Meg started to speak, but Kurt lifted his finger in a shushing motion. "We're selling the house, and that's all that needs to be said. On Friday night you're coming back with me. We'll hire someone to pack it up. Oh, and no funny business in between."

"Funny business?"

"Yeah, like the For Sale sign."

"What about it?"

"Don't be coy—it disappeared."

"It's gone? Well, I didn't touch it. Maybe some neighbor kid— "

"Meg," Kurt interrupted, "I found it in the basement—in the old coal room!"

Meg stood staring.

"Don't look so shocked."

She bristled at the insinuation. "How dare you, Kurt Rockwell!" Hard to ignite, her temper flared and burned brightly when it did. "I may not always do the right thing. I make my mistakes. But I can tell you one thing—I tell the truth! What about you? Are you truthful? You with your 'Buyer beware'?"

Kurt stood stunned by Meg. He had never seen her get so angry.

"Do you have moral integrity, Kurt?" Meg continued.

"What?" Kurt looked perplexed.

Meg paused, allowing a woman to pass them and enter the library. She hadn't meant for the subject to come up in this way, but it had.

"I'm talking about faithfulness, Kurt. You have not been the faithful husband!"

"Huh?" Kurt registered complete surprise. He drew in a sharp breath. "What are you talking about?"

"I'm talking about you. Tell me, just why did your first wife sue for divorce?"

He paled at once.

"Why?" Meg pressed.

Kurt tried to collect himself. "I—I was having an affair."

"Adultery."

He nodded. "Is that what this is about?"

"What's the cliché about leopards and their spots, Kurt? I bet you know that one."

"What do you mean? I can assure you, Meg, that— "

"I mean your sordid little affair with Valerie Miller, for God's sakes! Or was it just a little one-night stand? How many others have there been, Kurt?"

"Valerie Miller! Meg, the woman is— "

"I have a witness!"

"A witness—to what?"

"A romance in the White Hen! Then a rendezvous in her condo. Couldn't you be a little more discreet? And Valerie Miller! Let's throw in discerning, too!"

"Oh, for God's sake who told you this?"

"What difference can it make?"

"I want to know who!"

"And I want to know why!"

"Meg, it's not true! I've been faithful to you."

"Right. You know I could forgive you, Kurt, for a weak moment or a stupid choice. But not your lying to me. I won't!"

Meg spun around and hurried into the library.

Kurt stood numbed by the exchange that had just played out. He couldn't believe the turn his visit had taken. He had to talk to her, to settle this.

Yet, to go back in after her—there would be a scene, a very

public scene. And he had to get the car back to his friend Delaney in Chicago. More importantly, there was a late afternoon one-on-one meeting with the president of the hospital. He couldn't miss it, didn't dare.

And to complicate things, there were important meetings scheduled through the weekend. God only knows what spin Meg would put on that, he thought.

He moved toward the silver Lexus now, feeling more than ever that events were spinning out of control.

———⋄∘⋐⋑∘⋄———

Meg sat at her microfiche station, shaking with emotion. Sensing Miss Millicent's curious eyes upon her, she started working with the machine, praying that the woman would not come over. After a few minutes, she lifted her head and stared at nothing in particular.

She could not get the vision of Kurt's face out of her mind. At the mention of Valerie Miller's name, something had stirred in his expression. Something like recognition? Guilt? There *was* something to it, Meg thought now. Her heart sank.

It was true—or was it?

NINETEEN

KURT WAS NOT SURPRISED THAT Meg did not pick up the phone or answer his messages all day Friday. The intensive series of meetings with visiting bigwigs at the hospital precluded the usual end of the week trip to Hammond on the South Shore line.

On Saturday morning he tried again, from the condo and then upon arriving at work. Still no answer. And the phone machine was not operating. The frustration worked on his blood pressure. He knew no one on Springfield Street whom he could call—and even if he did, what would he say to them?

He would have to wait until he was able to get away early in the week.

At 10 a.m. Monday morning, Kurt dialed Wenonah Smythe from his office. He knew she worked three to elevens and hoped she would be awake by now.

She was having her coffee, she said.

"Wenonah, would it be all right if I come over for a short visit. I'd like to talk to you."

There was a pause, long enough for him to wonder if he hadn't been cut off.

"About Meg?" she asked at last. Her voice was oddly tentative, so unlike her.

"Yes."

"When?"

"In half an hour, if that's all right."

"Well—I guess so— "

He had taken her off guard, that was obvious. "Good. See you then."

After the goodbyes, he called Enterprise Rent-a-Car and set up a rental for 5:30 p.m. He wasn't about to screw around with the train today, and he needed a full size car to bring personal belongings back to Chicago. If Meg could be convinced to come back, her car would not be big enough.

Had he taken the train, he had to wonder if Meg would pick him up at the station. He had never seen her so angry. Would she agree to come back?

Kurt now put in a call to Doctor Krista Peterhof.

Yes, the doctor was in, he was told, but she was with a patient and could not be disturbed. The secretary took his name, saying the doctor would return the call later in the day.

Kurt asked that she call back after 11:30, expecting that he would be back from Wenonah's by then. The doctor would be given the message, he was told.

He slammed down the phone. *Disturbed, my ass! She should try my shoes.*

More frustration. He wanted to know what went on in their session, what frame of mind Meg was in, what advice the good doctor had given her.

⊸∘⊂✤∘⊂

Reaching for Wenonah's bell, he realized he was nervous and this surprised him. He had never been completely at ease with Wenonah, and he didn't know quite why. It wasn't her brash humor—he rather liked that. He couldn't quite put his finger on it.

Wenonah buzzed him in.

Kurt had never been in The Pattington, and he scarcely noticed the vintage ambiance now: the tiled vestibule, the wide stairway, the huge windows on each half landing, the scent of varnish and age.

Climbing the fourth flight, he thought maybe it was Wenonah's attitude toward him that put distance between them. And now, of course, he was on the defensive, and that was an unsettling thing.

"Hi," Wenonah said, her tone serious. She was dressed, but he could tell she had not been out of the shower long.

"Sorry for the short notice, Win."

"That's okay. I need to get up and take care of business. Morning TV is downright addictive, you know?"

"Can we sit?"

"Oh, sure. Sorry. Come on in. Want some coffee? It's still hot."

"No, thanks." Kurt sat on the sofa. The TV was on, but set on mute.

Wenonah settled into a lounge chair to the side and a bit removed. Her face was a mask that revealed little. She was nervous, too, he realized. She waited for him to speak.

Kurt drew in a long breath, then spoke. "Wenonah, Meg seems to think I've had an affair or am having one—or some damned thing."

He paused, assessing her. She didn't flinch. She didn't register surprise—only what?—a subtle discomfort? She was waiting for him to continue.

Kurt fully described Meg's accusation.

Wenonah simply took it in. And when he finished, she said bluntly: "And you think I'm that witness?"

He nodded. "I think it's a strong possibility. I know I used to see you at the White Hen, now and then. Hell—yes, I do think it."

Wenonah fastened her dark eyes on Kurt. "Look, I want your marriage to succeed. Meg is my best friend. She's very, very special, and I want to see her happy."

"Did you tell her those things?"

"I told her what I had seen and—believe me—it killed me to do so. I put it off as long as I could, but my conscience finally won out."

"Your conscience?" Kurt turned sarcastic.

"I gave her the information, just what I had seen, without any editorial commentary. In fact, I cautioned her that what I had seen was merely circumstantial, that it may, after all, have been innocent."

"I see." Kurt's eyes moved from Wenonah to the TV. Some soap opera played silently.

"Was it, Kurt? Innocent?"

Kurt was taken aback by her boldness. Her initial nervousness had made him forget for the moment how direct she could be. He looked at her squarely in the face. Her gaze was as direct as her question. "Yes," he said, finally, "nothing happened that night, or ever."

Wenonah nodded, but the hint of skepticism lay like a delicate scrim over her eyes. "I hope you understand it was something I had to do."

"Point taken. And I'll defend myself. Nothing happened! I love Meg. And this could not have happened at a worse time! You have no idea, Win."

Wenonah's face folded into an expression of concern. "Has anything happened—since that worker fell?"

Kurt went into the details as he knew them. He brought Wenonah up to date on the construction worker's mishap and the child-ghost the man said he had seen, the visit to the nursing home and the death of the Clinton woman. The longer the litany became, the more he felt he was doing the right thing in insisting Meg move back to Chicago.

"How terrible," Wenonah whispered. She had paled.

"I feel she's in some kind of danger, Win. She's got to stop pursuing this—whatever the hell it is. If there's anything you can do, any way you can influence her, I'd appreciate it."

Wenonah sat forward in her chair. "Kurt, she needs to move back!"

"Don't I know it? I'm going to do everything I can to get her back tonight."

"I'll call her."

"Would you? Today? That'd be great."

"Yes."

"And maybe put in a good word for me?"

Wenonah smiled.

"I don't know if you believe me, Win— "

"I believe you love Meg, Kurt, or you wouldn't be here. I'll let her know that."

Kurt wanted to stay, wanted to shake Wenonah's doubts free, but he was at a loss as to how. Instead, he smiled, stood, thanked her, and left.

Kurt swore aloud when his secretary told him he had missed Doctor Peterhof's call by five minutes.

He called her office immediately. Too late, she was already in conference with another patient.

"Yes," he was told, the doctor would return his call at her earliest convenience. He hung up and cursed again.

At one o'clock, he was on the third floor of the hospital when he was paged to the phone. He rushed to pick it up at the nurses' station.

"Mr. Rockwell?" It was a woman's voice.

"Doctor Peterhof? Yes."

"Who? No this is Mrs. Shaw. Is that you, Mr. Rockwell?"

Damn! Of course, the voice came across now as familiar. "I'm sorry, Mrs. Shaw. I was expecting someone else."

"Listen, Mr. Rockwell, we've got a real problem out here. Do you know the sign has been removed again?"

"Has it? Well, not to worry—I'll be out this evening."

"Well, that's not the most important thing right now."

"What do you mean?"

"Your wife doesn't answer the phone or the door. I've been out to the house twice today, once last night."

Kurt could feel the heat of his blood pumping up through his neck and to his temples. "You'll have cooperation once I get there, Mrs. Shaw, I promise."

"It's more immediate than that, Mr. Rockwell, or I wouldn't have called you at work. The Robbins are still very much interested in the place. But we need to do business this afternoon."

"Oh, come on— "

"No, really. They've got a six o'clock plane out of O'Hare to Orlando. It's the start of a three-week vacation. They're not about to change their plans."

"And?"

"And they'll write a check out for a deposit and sign a proposal on the spot if they can see the house again—and talk to you or your wife."

"About?"

"I suspect they want to know why you're giving it up so soon."

"I see. Okay, Mrs. Shaw, I'm renting a car today. I'll get the time moved up and come out as soon as possible. I'll meet you at the house, say at three?"

"Fine. You know, your wife could assure them instead if I could only get a hold of her."

"No, no, Mrs. Shaw." *Good God, no!* "That's okay, Mrs. Shaw. See you at three."

"All right, then."

Kurt arranged for the car and was just about to leave work to pick it up when Doctor Krista Peterhof called back.

The strange voice and accent threw him for a moment—he had actually forgotten about the call.

"I wanted to know about Meg, Doctor Peterhof," he explained.

"She is a fine young woman, Mr. Rockwell."

"That I know, Doctor. Can—can you tell me what went on in your session, what your assessment is?"

There was a pause at the other end before the doctor spoke. "Meg is stable, if that's what you mean. I can say that much."

"Yes, but— "

"As for what went on in the session, it is not my policy to speak to others—even husbands, Mr. Rockwell—about a patient's session."

"But this is rather unusual, wouldn't you say, Doctor Peterhof? I mean, she's not really a patient even, is she? She went to you for information about the holographic thing."

"Yes, that's true."

"She told you about the spirits? The dreams?"

"She did."

"Did you advise her?"

"I think she should tell you what went on. This is a case in which I would neither try to persuade nor dissuade. Why aren't you asking *her*, Mr. Rockwell?"

Too embarrassed to admit he and Meg were at odds, he avoided her question. "Don't you think that she may be putting herself and the baby in danger?"

"I doubt that, Mr. Rockwell. And if that is what you think, what are you doing in Chicago?"

Kurt was stunned by the question. And angry. "Because I have a job to maintain, Doctor."

"I see. So do I, Mr. Rockwell, and I am even now keeping a patient waiting, so you must excuse me. Let me just tell you that Meg is empowered to study her options and make the right decisions for herself. Goodbye, Mr. Rockwell."

"What do you mean— " he blurted loudly.

But the woman had already hung up.

The Chevy Caprice was comfortable. At ten miles over the limit, Kurt sped off the Dan Ryan onto the Bishop Ford Expressway. He wished he could call Meg. The hospital had issued him a cell phone, but he seldom took it from his desk drawer. He had little use for it, and besides, it would do little good because Meg had turned hers in when she quit the hospital. He vowed now to start using his as a matter of course, and he would get one for her, as well.

His blood pressure had come down a bit. What had that pompous doctor meant, he wondered, about Meg's being *empowered* to make decisions for herself? She claimed she hadn't advised her, yet somehow she seemed to imply that she had empowered Meg. What the hell did it mean?

Something, too, about his meeting with Wenonah was eating away at him. Okay, so he didn't convince her, so what? It didn't matter. She would at least urge Meg to leave the house.

But it *did* matter. He knew what was wrong—he hadn't convinced her he was truthful because he hadn't *felt* truthful. And Wenonah, whatever her faults, was as perceptive as radar.

His thoughts went back to that night at the White Hen.

Valerie Miller had always been flirtatious toward him, and with Meg's living out in Hammond and his staying in the city during the week, she took the first opportunity that came along.

In the White Hen it had been her move, he assured himself. She was downright pushy. *Gee, it's so sad that, well, here we are buying our own little deli dinners, and we have nothing but TV for company, not even pets, and here we are living on the same floor, for goodness sakes and, well, wouldn't it be enjoyable and perfectly innocent if we shared a bite to make up for the loneliness of the night?*

Kurt wouldn't lie to himself. He was no more innocent than she. He had played the game, too, dropping off his briefcase at the condo and changing into dockers and a polo shirt before knocking on the door across the hall.

He knew exactly what Valerie had in mind. However, as the evening went on, he began to feel differently.

It wasn't that Valerie became annoying or unattractive in any way. She was vibrant and sexy.

But she wasn't Meg. He loved Meg, more now than before they were married. Being with Valerie—it was like, what was the point? What was he doing there? How would he feel afterwards? Would it be worth it? He knew the answer.

Fortunately, the woman wasn't quite pushy enough and gave him time for second thoughts, time to formulate and execute a retreat. He played the wide-eyed innocent, going on with their share-a-meal game ad nauseum—until he could make a hasty exit.

She hadn't spoken to him since.

So he could shout his innocence. And he *was* innocent. But not completely. Wenonah had read the guilt that morning; he was sure of it.

Meg must have read it, too.

Kurt concluded that he would have to let out the whole story, sparing nothing.

The house, Mrs. Shaw, the Robbins were second in priority. His main concerns now were Meg, her safety, her view of him, and their child.

Things will turn out okay, he told himself as he turned off the expressway.

Kurt Rockwell was not one for premonitions, but something deep within gnawed at him, telling him things would not turn out okay at all. Not at all.

TWENTY

IT RAINED ON MONDAY IN Hammond. The funeral for Bernadine Clinton was pitifully small. And sad. Few relations, fewer friends.

Meg sat with Miss Millicent. It was all she could do to stay to the end. Despite Doctor Peterhof's reassurance, she still felt a sense of personal responsibility for the woman's death.

In the afternoon Meg arrived at the Calumet Room, having completed the last two health care visits. Allowing for the possibility that she would be returning to Chicago, she had purposely taken no others this week or the next. And then there was the more immediate need to solve the riddle of the house and the Reichart family.

The pressure from Kurt to move would be great. She had not written off the marriage even though she had seen in his denial—felt it, too—something phony. What was it? And the phone message he had left about the weekend meetings—was there any truth in that?

Meg knew one thing for sure: they had a child on the way. Somehow, they would survive the crisis. They must.

She attempted to clear her mind, settling into her usual spot, thinking only how much she needed results. Today. The first order of business was to find out about Alicia's demise, then retrace her steps through her research, looking for more specifics on Claude's death. There had to be more than a simple obit.

A little after two o'clock, she found the obituary of Alicia Reichart. She had died November 12, 1934, at the age of fifty-four. Her death notice merited several lines, and was included in the section that noted the passing of city and national figures. No picture.

After detailing her marriage into the prestigious Reichart family, the account saved the shocker for the end of the single paragraph. *Mrs. Reichart died at the LaPorte County Asylum, after a stay of eleven years.*

Meg's stomach tightened. *Sweet Jesus!* She felt suddenly sick to her stomach. And in her mind's eye, she pictured the woman hanging from knotted bed sheets strung over pipes that ran along the ceiling of her tiny cell. She didn't know why this vision came to her, didn't know whether it could actually reflect the woman's end. How could it?

And yet, Meg believed it.

She was overcome with the sense of tragedy, wrongs done, opportunities lost. After so much tragedy, she thought, to spend the final decade of one's life in an insane asylum! Meg struggled to take in breath.

Then the thought: What kind of a spirit or soul evolves from such a life, such losses, and such an end? Not a spirit, Meg thought, remembering her talk with Krista Peterhof. A ghost.

What was she to expect from the ghost of Alicia Reichart?

———◦◦◦———

Kurt arrived at the house with fifteen minutes to spare before Mrs. Shaw and the Robbins were due.

The sign *was* missing again.

Meg wasn't home. No surprise there. Probably at the library.

He was glad for her absence. The proposal would be written,

signed, and the sale in the proverbial bag by the time she got home. No catches, thank you.

The house was cool and quiet. Rex strutted by toward the kitchen and his food, ignoring Kurt, almost making a point of it. "Little beggar," Kurt mumbled.

Of course, Meg had to sign the proposal, too. But that would be done only in his company, with no chance of the deal being scuttled.

Smooth as good bourbon, this wretched experience would be over.

Kurt walked the length of the house now—past Rex, crunching at his bowl—to the enclosed rear stairwell that ran from the basement to an outside door off the drive, to the kitchen door, and then to the second floor. He went down and opened the basement door, red as a fire hydrant. He didn't bother to close it behind him—he had closed the kitchen door, preventing Rex from wandering down into the labyrinthine basement.

Most of the seven or eight rooms were piled with stuff. Just looking at what needed to be done in order to move back to Chicago was daunting and depressing. He would try to arrange for the movers to come next week. He would have to rent storage, to be sure. He walked through the laundry room, then into the furnace room, pulling the strings that lighted the bare bulbs. He came to the coal room at the front of the house. It was damper than he remembered, downright cold, in fact. His shoes made a crunching sound as he crossed the floor made up of crushed bits of coal delivered decades before.

He saw the For Sale sign leaning against the front wall. The light from the glass block window above it revealed it to be in the same spot he had found it on the Friday before. Finding no string for the light, he reached up to turn the bulb in the porcelain socket above him.

At his touch the bulb flashed on for just a moment before it flared—and exploded. Shards of fragile glass rained on and about him.

"Holy Shit!" Kurt cried, pulling his hand back to safety. He was blinded for a few seconds. The thing had scared the hell out of him. He was certain he hadn't been too rough—the thing had simply come apart in his hand like an eggshell.

How to explain it?

Brushing glass bits from his hair, he moved forward now, stepping on the crunching, grinding glass. He was lucky he hadn't been cut.

He had no sooner grasped the sign and turned around when he heard a noise from one of the other rooms.

The laundry room. The washer had come on.

"Meg?" he called. Had she come in?

She would certainly be aware that he was there. The Caprice was in the driveway. The other basement lights were on. Was she trying to give him a good scare? Was she being funny? If so, it was a poor joke.

"Meg!"

He walked slowly now back through the windowless furnace room. It was dark here—the light he had turned on near the hot water heater had gone out. He reached up and let out a cry. The broken bulb there cut through the underside of his fore finger. He pulled it back and instinctively sucked at the blood. How had this bulb been broken? He felt the hackles at the back of his neck rise.

He passed quickly out and into the laundry room. Here there was moderate light afforded by the glass block windows over the ancient laundry tubs. The bulb here, too—burning a few minutes before—had gone out. He heard the sound of glass grinding under his shoes and knew that bulb had met the same fate as the other two. How could they all have exploded at the same time? Was there some science to it he was ignorant of?

The stink of dead flowers was in the air, but there was more to concern him now. Kurt stood staring stupidly at the washer. Set on Cold wash/Cold rinse, it was filling up with water.

"Meg!" he screamed. But he sensed she was not to blame.

He cautiously walked to the machine.

Was this some strange electrical short going on? Dare he even touch it? Would he get a shock—or worse?

Nonsense, he thought, summoning the strength to reach for and slowly lift the lid, the lid he was almost certain had not been down when he passed through the room a few minutes before.

He peered inside.

Water only, filling fast.

Weird. He reached out to pull the Stop button.

His hand had not quite connected with it when he saw the timing knob for the dryer—just to his right—turn, slowly, steadily, its gears clicking as it rotated.

At the sixty-minute mark, the knob pressed in toward the control panel, then was released, setting the dryer in motion.

Kurt stood there dumb, heart pounding like a hammer in his chest, his mind fending off panic as he listened to the washer start to agitate now.

What the hell is happening here?

The initial fear started to dissipate as he thought how absurd this all was. Here he stood watching two machines with lives and wills of their own. And Mrs. Shaw with his ticket out of Hammond would be arriving any minute. The thought buoyed him now, and he reached out to shut down the machines.

His hand moved toward the four-way receptacle, then stopped.

Neither the washer nor the dryer was plugged in! He looked to the floor behind the machines. The cords lay useless on the cement.

Suddenly, above the din of the two machines, he heard a high, melodic sound from above—in the dining room. The doorbell.

Mrs. Shaw! The repetition of the ringing told him that it had likely been rung a couple of times already.

Kurt sprinted now for the back room and the stairway.

The red basement door loomed in front of him like a stop sign. It was closed. Fully closed! He knew he hadn't closed it. Who had? Someone—something—had closed it!

He stopped in his tracks, heart pumping, pounding.

What the hell is at work down here?

"What's going on?" he shouted.

He heard the doorbell sound again.

He rushed the door. Just as he reached the darkened brass handle, he heard a noise on the other side.

The sound of the bolt being slid into place.

His face pulsed hotly. *What is happening?*

"Meg!" he called.

No response.

"Who's there?" he shouted.

He knew the door had been bolted on the other side, yet he instinctively reached and pulled just the same.

Locked. He pulled again. A strong door, strong lock.

The doorbell chimes had gone silent, he realized.

Mrs. Shaw! He had to get her attention before they left.

He turned and ran again into the laundry room, into the furnace room, slowing a bit now in the dark, and then into the coal room.

He ran to the glass block window, calling out the real estate woman's name. He pulled a plastic milk crate to the window, turned it on end—dumping out papers and books in the process.

Standing on the crate, he struck at the window.

"Help!" he shouted. "Mrs. Shaw! Down here!"

When he paused and put his face flush to the window, looking to the right, he could see a bit of the front porch. He could see the red of a woman's shoe.

He called out again.

And again.

169

His knuckles were sore from rapping against the window. The glass was thick, too thick.

Panic rising within him, he jumped from the crate and searched for something that would resound against the glass blocks. He found a rusty pair of grass shears.

Climbing onto the crate again, he looked before he started striking. He saw feet descending the few stairs at the front porch, then disappearing as they moved down.

They were leaving!

Good God, don't leave!

He bashed the clippers against the window, simultaneously screaming at the top of his lungs.

The old metal against the thick glass made more noise than his hands had done, but the trio had already moved too far away. He could make out their blurred figures now—two women and one man—down on the sidewalk near the street.

In a rage Kurt threw the clippers across the room. He cursed violently.

He turned to the window again, motioning wildly with his arms. *Just look back! Just one of you look back, just once. You'll see. You'll see!*

The figures fell into profile now and were moving away to their cars.

"Don't leave, damn it! Don't leave!"

He stopped waving, fully spent. He slowly turned around, his back slumping against the cold wall.

What am I in for now? He looked about at the shadows and a kind of despair he had never known took over. Here I am, a prisoner in my own basement, he thought, and the Robbins are off to frickin' Disneyland. We've lost the sale.

As if punctuate his thought, the plastic crate beneath his feet shot out from under him now with some unnatural force and flew like a cannonball against the opposite wall.

Kurt crashed to the coal-strewn floor.

TWENTY—ONE

THE DISCOVERY OF ALICIA REICHART'S 1934 obituary prompted Meg to backtrack to the years 1908 to 1911. She wanted more on Claude.

The Calumet Room would close soon. The ten-minute warning had already come.

Suddenly the Reichart name caught her eye. In a 1910 article on what constituted the society page, the talents of Claude Reichart, the pride of his parents and their hopes for the future were all enumerated. It was much like the other article Meg had found previously. But with a difference—here there was a picture, fairly crisp.

Meg sat forward in her chair, rigid and chilled to the bone.

She recognized the little angelic bespectacled face as the one she had seen in the coach house window on the day she and Kurt had first viewed the house. She was absolutely certain. And it was also the face of the boy—spirit or ghost?—who had chased Rex upstairs and out onto the balcony.

"Five minutes," whispered Miss Millicent, startling her. "Find something, my dear?"

"Yes, a picture of Claude Reichart."

"Oh?" The woman advanced and hovered over Meg. "Goodness, what an attractive young boy. Look how full of life he was! And to think how short his life was to be! When did you say he passed on?"

But he didn't pass on, Meg thought, *not really. That's the whole point.* "1911," she answered now, "just a few months after this picture was taken."

"Isn't that a shame?"

It was a shame. More and more, Meg's heart was weeping for the tragedies of Claude and Alicia Reichart. She felt their losses more keenly every day, it seemed.

"Shouldn't you be finishing up for the day?" Miss Millicent asked, glancing purposefully at her watch.

"I will. I promise. I just know there must be something here about his death."

"If it's been here all these years, dear, I'm certain it'll wait till next time. Mystery is a spice, isn't it?"

No, it *can't* wait, Meg wanted to say as Miss Millicent went about the business of closing up.

Meg found it now—the keystone of her search. She had not been focusing much on the newspaper's front pages, but as the front page for July 17th flashed by, she sighted something familiar. She brought the page back.

There was the same picture of Claude Reichart, just below a two-column story at the right of the page. The caption read:

REICHART BARN BURNS ONE DEAD

Meg shivered at the thought of a child burnt to death in a fire— and, somehow—this child especially. She was for the moment a vessel, and sadness filled her to the brim.

Meg had no time to read the details.

"I'm afraid it is time," Miss Millicent said. She had her coat on. "Did you find something else, Meg?"

"Yes, something," Meg answered, pressing the button for the

copy machine—and relieved that the woman was too involved in closing the room for the day to inquire further.

Meg placed the two important finds of the day in her purse. She had, she thought, the final piece of the puzzle. Putting it together would now be up to her.

During the drive home, Meg's thoughts shifted to Kurt.

How were they to keep their marriage from unraveling?

He had been leaving several desperate sounding messages on the machine daily, pleading his innocence. Yet her heart had told her it wasn't innocence she read in his eyes when he addressed the Valerie Miller issue.

She turned into the driveway and for once allowed herself to study the old coach house as the car glided toward it.

What was this aversion she had to it? Was it merely that face at the window she had seen months ago?

There was no face at that window now. The structure defined the word *dilapidated*. The low stone and mortar wall and foundation seemed to be in better shape than the rest of the wooden structure's two stories and hip roof. The carriage doors in the back had been boarded up years before, and those in front had been replaced in the 50s or 60s with cheap metal overhead doors—rusty, broken, and useless now. On the second floor, where living quarters had been fashioned, four windows faced the drive—two for the bedroom and two for the little living room.

Meg and Kurt had planned to have the building demolished. She would be glad to see it gone—if they could still somehow keep the house. The thought of losing the house put her on edge. It was a dark thought, and she put it out of her mind.

Meg was out of the car before it dawned on her that there was another car in the drive, next to hers. She didn't recognize it and couldn't imagine whose it was. No one seemed to be about the grounds.

Had Kurt borrowed a car again? It wasn't likely he'd come out on a Monday. Meg thought of Mrs. Shaw, and ruled her out because she owned a red Lumina—but maybe it belonged to one of her clients.

Had Kurt given Mrs. Shaw keys to the house? Meg burned at the thought.

She let herself in the side door. Five curving steps would take her up to the kitchen door.

She paused now in the cool hallway, listening. And then she was nearly overpowered by the scent of violets, decaying violets. She was only just taking this in when a terrible, bone-chilling cold entered her—and then passed out of her, moving upward in the direction of the first floor door. It had come from the basement steps. She stood, motionless, thoughtless. She felt as if she had been violated, raped.

A muffled cry suddenly wrenched her to alertness. The cry of a man.

"Who is it?" she called, her voice breaking. She clutched her purse to her chest, her hand already searching for her mace.

"Meg!"

The voice was Kurt's!

"Yes! Where are *you*?"

"Down here! In the basement, Meg!"

Meg turned right, descended two steps, turned left, and moved down toward the bright red basement door.

"Meg!" Kurt called again.

"Coming!" As she came to the door, she could not believe what she saw. The door was bolted on her side.

She pushed back the bolt, and Kurt pulled the door open.

She had never seen him look frightened before. Not ever. He was white as porcelain, and terror clouded the blue eyes. Cobwebs clung to his dark hair. Blood spattered his white shirt.

"Oh, Meg, thank God!" His breathing was labored. He leaned against a small chest-size freezer that stood near the door. "I . . . didn't know what to do . . . these damn glass block windows. My God, it's like a prison down here!"

Meg didn't hesitate, moving toward him in her concern, grasping onto his arm. "You're hurt!"

"It's—it's just a little cut—from the light bulb.—Let's get upstairs."

"Are you all right?"

"Upstairs, Meg!"

She held onto his arm as they moved up the stairs. He was trembling, she realized.

They seated themselves at the dining room table, and the details of Kurt's ordeal poured out.

As Kurt became less frightened, Meg inwardly became more frightened. It was her fault. She had done this. She had opened herself up to this. If only she had known she would be putting others in jeopardy.

His story told, Kurt rested in the first floor bedroom while Meg prepared a quick meal. She knew he wasn't sleeping. She knew they were both taking inventory and stockpiling weapons for the struggle to come, the struggle between themselves. The struggle about the house.

They hardly spoke at their meal. Meg ate slowly, surreptitiously glancing at Kurt, not wishing to bring up the subject of the house, and thinking again and again about the old newspaper article in her purse, the one she still had not yet read.

The turkey pastrami and cheese sandwich and the beef barley soup seemed to restore Kurt. Meg could tell he was embarrassed about what had happened, how he had behaved. She knew his male pride had been damaged.

He sat watching her; he had finished first and appeared to be waiting for her to finish. The moment she dreaded was coming.

Still, it was she who spoke first. "Feel better?" She pushed away her unfinished soup.

"We're getting out of here, Meg. Tonight."

Meg studied him. She had made the serve and his volley now was direct and lethal. The terror was gone from his eyes, and his face was set with determination.

"Look, Kurt. I don't need to ask why. Not after this afternoon. And I can't blame you— "

"Meg, you're not going to say you want to stay?"

"It's not that I want to stay— "

"Then it's settled."

"Not quite, Kurt." If only she could communicate her need, make him understand.

"What is it? It's about last Friday, isn't it?"

"No, that's not— "

"Yes, it is. . . . I went to see Wenonah today."

"You did what?"

"Her part in this wasn't too hard to figure out—and I can see how she arrived at her circumstantial evidence. And, Meg, I wasn't completely truthful."

Meg had been prepared for another denial, but she felt her heart catch now at his last admission. What was he going to reveal? She looked away, resigned to hear the worst.

"Valerie Miller is a flirt, Meg," Kurt was saying.

"And not unattractive."

"All right, attractive enough. I'm not going to make excuses for myself. You need to hear me out. That night that Wenonah saw us . . . we did go into her apartment, and I have to admit the intention was for more than a little deli supper."

Meg turned back to him, tears brimming in her eyes.

"I did," he continued, "make a terrible decision. Of that I'm guilty. But thank God, I had time for second thoughts. I thought how my first marriage had fallen apart. You were right on about that—I was having an affair when Julie found out. The affair meant nothing—nothing!—but it destroyed my marriage. I became determined not to let history repeat. And I can tell you that I got the hell out of Valerie Miller's condo as fast as I could."

"Oh, Kurt— "

"You can rip at me all you want, Meg, but I've been faithful to you. I want this marriage to work. I want you with me, Meg. And the baby."

Kurt took Meg's hand now, his eyes fastening on hers. "I have been faithful, Meg—with the exception of one mental lapse.— Hell, even Jimmy Carter lusted in his heart."

Meg would not validate the humor relief he was attempting. "You were going to act on it."

Kurt's eyes lowered to half-mast. "But I didn't, Meg. I didn't." The eyelids slowly lifted now. "Do you believe me?"

Meg sensed that this was the truth, and relief streamed through her. "Yes," she said. Kurt squeezed her hand, and she returned the pressure.

"Thanks, Meg." He leaned over and hugged her to him.

It was an awkward gesture, but she appreciated it, nonetheless.

He drew back now. "Then you'll come back with me tonight?"

Meg looked into his hopeful eyes and shook her head, sadly. "Not yet, Kurt."

"Meg— "

"I've still got some things to figure out."

"About the house?"

"Yes."

"The . . . spirits?"

"Yes."

"Are you crazy? Why? What's making you stay here?"

"I don't know. A feeling—an impulse voice—that's what Doctor Peterhof calls it. I feel that somehow I can set things right."

"To keep the house?"

"Maybe—but, well, maybe I can do some good."

"For people who have been dead for years? Decades? Come on, Meg!'"

"I need just a little more time in the house. If that doesn't do it, I'll come back to the city next week and never look back."

"And if it is enough time, if it does do it, what then? You expect to *stay* here? Do you think I would spend another night in the house after this afternoon?"

Meg shrugged. "I can't think of all the things ahead of us. We could at least sell the house with clear consciences. I know I need only a few days."

"Even if I don't—can't—stay?"

Meg pursed her lips. "Even if."

Kurt's face flushed with anger at her resoluteness. She watched as he tried to reign in his temper.

"Then I'm wasting my time," he said, pulling his hand away and standing. "I have to pack my clothes."

Meg could think of nothing to say, nothing to resolve their differences.

His temper tore free of its mooring now. "I swear to God the only way I'll come back to this house is to sign the sale papers. Or to pick you up! And you'll have to call me, Meg!" He was shouting now. "You'll have to call *me*! I won't call or come begging!"

Meg held back her tears. Still, her mouth would not move.

When the silence became too much to bear, Meg picked up the dishes and went into the kitchen. She heard Kurt moving off toward the bedroom.

Meg went back to the dining table and sat, despondent that she had hurt him. Oh, it was hurt all right that sparked his temper and provoked his ultimatum. Hurt that she didn't choose to be with him, hurt that she had chosen the house over him. If only he would understand—could understand—what compelled her. But how could he?—when she didn't understand it herself.

After Kurt had piled his belongings at the front door, after he had carried them to the car, after he had called out a goodbye that begged her to relent, she thought of running to the door and calling to him. She thought of leaving with him.

Now the car was backing down the drive, and Meg stirred herself from her lethargy at the table. She found herself hurrying—not to the door—but to the living room where she had left her purse.

In it was the article on Claude Reichart's death.

TWENTY—TWO

KURT HAD TAKEN THE LESS traveled Chicago Skyway out of Indiana instead of the Bishop Ford Expressway. He couldn't remember having made a conscious decision to do so. The Caprice emptied into the Dan Ryan expressway now, and the lights, noise, and motion awakened him to the foggy state he was in. He sat up straight, opened the window. One had to drive with all senses alerted when on the infamous Dan Ryan.

Why had he taken the Skyway? He could not even remember paying the $2.50 in tolls—the reason why it was the road less traveled.

His life was in a tailspin. Things that he thought mattered—Mrs. Shaw, The Robbins, unloading the house, even the spirit of the house—fell into perspective. Even his career, or maybe especially his career, surfaced in his mind for what it was—a job with a sharklike nature of overseeing cutting and slashing, a job that made for him a comfortable living, as long as he played the current corporate game of health care, an industry—yes, that's what it was now!—that precluded any humanitarian thoughts or concern for the health of patients.

What mattered were Meg and his child. These were real to him. And he had screwed up again. How had he managed to do it?

He thought of turning around and going back. He wished that he could, but he couldn't. He had set an ultimatum for Meg that he regretted now, bitterly. What had he been thinking? Did he expect her to come running out to the drive, make him stop, and accompany him to Chicago?

No, Meg was stronger than that. He was still learning how strong she was.

The Caprice was approaching Lake Shore Drive now. He would be at the condo in ten minutes.

What's keeping me from turning back?

———⟡———

Meg sat quietly in the bay, but her body was tense, her mind on edge. She had read the article twice. It detailed the burning of the barn that had been repurposed to use as the Reichart garage with servants' quarters overhead. The wooden structure burned down to the four-foot-high stone and mortar wall and foundation. Claude Reichart, a nine-year-old child pianist and composer, died in the blaze. An investigation of the fire's cause was being undertaken by the fire and police departments. No one could explain Claude's presence in the barn. It had been, a grieving Mrs. Alicia Reichart told the reporter, out of bounds for her son.

Mrs. Reichart had been hosting a luncheon at the time for the members of the Presbyterian Ladies Society. Claude, already well known in Northern Indiana as a musical prodigy, was to play the piano for the ladies after the meal.

At the first alarm, the ladies ran to the verandah and watched in horror as the barn was consumed by the blaze. They could, Mrs. Julia Mulvihill said, see Claude's face and form at the upper window before the smoke inside became too thick. "He was there one moment," she said, "and then he was gone."

The story was disturbing and heart-rending.

Meg remembered now what Krista had said about dual unities—that such a manifestation was common with mothers and newborns, but could also apply to a mother and older child if the bond was especially close, or if one or both deaths were traumatic, perhaps leaving things unfulfilled. The likelihood of this phenomenon might even be further increased, she had said, if the mother witnessed the child's death.

Alicia had witnessed her son's death, and it had been no bedside vigil where some measure of preparation and closure might have been possible. Alicia had watched her first-born—a child with the talents of one in a generation—burn to death before her very eyes.

Good God! Was it any wonder after that and the subsequent loss of her husband and twins to influenza that the woman died in an asylum?

What a tormented soul she must have been. *Or is!*

Meg became convinced that the experiences with the spirits—or ghosts—of the boy and his mother did suggest a dual unity.

But what, if anything, did they want from her?

How could they be put to rest?

Meg read the article again, and not long after, a profound tiredness came over her. She fell asleep in her chair at about nine o'clock in the evening.

She dreamt.

Afterward she would recall that it started with a soundless dream she had had before. She was seated in a small, crowded room. It was daylight and the heat was almost tropical. People's faces turned to her occasionally. Women's faces. Women with large decorous hats and broad smiles behind waving fans.

All at once the women were on their feet, and Meg found herself in the crush as they pushed toward a doorway. Their faces bespoke panic and horror, but their screams from open mouths were as from a silent film.

Meg was on a porch now and looking up at a burning building—a barn. She would recall the dream as one in black and white, like the silents—except for the flames bursting in hues of yellow, orange, and red, flames that rose from the building like fluttering tropical birds.

Then she saw the face at the single window high up on the barn's façade. The face from the news articles: Claude Reichart's face. Even in her dream she recognized that this haunting visage was the same she had witnessed that first day in the window of the coach house.

Her heart contracted, and she reached out to the boy in the window, the boy with the huge sorrowful eyes, like those in the old Keane prints. Her mouth opened to call, to scream, but her efforts were voiceless. Her world spun, its bottom dropping out. This was the same sense of losing someone precious to her that she had experienced in her previous dreams. It was a depthless heartache.

Suddenly, the dream shifted, as dreams so inexplicably do. She was in the barn's hayloft, staring down a ladder to where a man moved about in the gloom. She was afraid to go down, afraid to approach the man. He seemed sinister, dangerous.

She lay down, curled herself into a ball, sniffing at the familiar smell of hay, feeling a bit more secure.

The dream jumped again. She was on her feet. Dark smoke was billowing up the opening that held the ladder she could no longer see. She could not go down.

The heat was intense. She was coughing now, choking. No flames yet up here. But soon, she prayed, they would be climbing to the hayloft in their attempt to reach her.

No—they would not reach her in time. She was going to die, she knew it!

She stumbled to the window. She wiped at the filthy glass, tried to pound at the panes, tried to break them. But whose hands were these? Whose arms?

Why, they were a child's!

She looked down, seemed to see a crowd of faces looking up at her. Did they see her? Wasn't anyone going to help her? If the window somehow opened, could she jump? *They're going to think I started the fire!*

She looked straight down to the ground.

The smoke, the heat, the vertigo overtook her now, and she felt herself falling . . . falling . . .

But it was the pain of her skin being singed by the flames that danced around her that awakened her, her head snapping back against the high back of the wicker chair.

She had perfect recall and knew immediately what had happened. Reading the article had prompted her to tap into the 1911 memories of the fire. First, as in all previous dreams, she experienced Alicia Reichart's memories. But then—and this made her shudder—she had somehow tapped into Claude's, as well.

These were not merely imaginings inspired by the article. They were full of details not in the article, details that made her believe she had envisioned the scenes as they unfolded in life ninety years before. The most haunting of these new details was the presence of the man on the first floor of the barn, a man she somehow *knew* to be responsible for the fire and for Claude's death.

This seemed to validate the notion of a dual unity—mother and son. Meg became aware of the familiar smell of decaying violets— the odor she had experienced often after the dreams, during and after the balcony mishap—even Kurt had smelled it!—and after the death of Bernadine Clinton. It was no doubt Alicia Reichart's favorite flower or fragrance.

But now—acrid, stronger, and more disturbing—came the smell of ash, something burnt. Meg had been aware of it only once before—the night she climbed the stairs following the apparition of the boy that had chased Rex. It made sense now and her stomach revolted at the realization. It was Claude's smell—that of human ash, burnt flesh. A little boy burnt to death.

Did the commingling of the two very separate smells further underscore the dual unity theory?

Meg went to the bedroom to find a business card she thought she had tossed into the top drawer. She said a little prayer of thanks that it was there—and that a home number was scribbled on the back.

She hurried to the dining room, picked up the phone and started to dial.

She paused before finishing, thought a moment, and hung up.

She picked up the phone and dialed a different number.

"Ravensfield Hospital."

"The Emergency Room, please."

No verbal response, just a click. Then ringing.

A woman picked up. "ER."

"Wenonah Smythe, please."

She was on the line in a few seconds.

"Listen, Wenonah, would it be a terrible hardship for you to come out here? To stay overnight?"

"Why?" Wenonah sounded worried. "What's happened?"

"Nothing much, yet anyway."

"Where's Kurt?"

"He was here, but he's gone back to the condo."

"I see."

Meg knew Wenonah was trying to fill in the pieces without probing too much. "It's not as bad as you think—between Kurt and me."

"Oh."

"I just need you here."

"Are you in danger?"

"No, I don't think so."

"You don't sound all that convincing. Can I come after my shift—we're swamped with crazies here. Full moon, you know."

"That's fine," Meg said. "You're off at eleven?"

"Yeah—but I'll have to stop at home and grab some clothes."

"No," Meg blurted. "I'll supply you with whatever you need. Please come out directly after work."

"Listen, Meg, I could try to get off now— "

"No, no! That's okay. See ya soon, Win."

"Bye."

Meg picked up the business card, turned it over, and quickly dialed again.

"Hello?"

"Dr. Peterhof? I mean Krista."

"Yes?"

"Meg Rockwell."

"Meg! How good to hear from you!"

"I'm sorry to call you at home—and so late. I didn't wake you, did I?"

"Goodness, no! What is it, Meg?"

"Well, I know you're going to think me odd, but I need some clarification on the dual unity thing."

"Okay . . . are you all right?"

"Yes, if you could just explain it again— "

"Certainly. Dual unity is a transpersonal relationship that connects one on a very deep level with another. The experience can occur with mothers and their babies, or during periods of great emotion or shock. Yoga can help facilitate it, as well as certain drugs. It's possible for one person to feel as if he—or she—is someone else."

"Might one identify with someone dead?"

"Undoubtedly."

"I see."

"In a weaker form this element of the holotropic mind is probably more of an empathy."

"And in the strongest form?"

"Well, I suppose it could almost become a kind of possession."

"And might someone identify with more than one person or—ghost? Simultaneously?"

"Yes, absolutely. In fact, I went to Dachau a few years ago and experienced a rather common form of this dual unity, myself. I walked up and down rows of razed cellblocks, crying hysterically.

The sense of loss and grief I felt is indescribable, Meg. Unspeakable. For the time I was there, I felt the terrible pain of those tragic souls who suffered and died there. For a time, I became them."

Meg let out a little gasp.

"Are you all right, Meg?"

"Yes—fine."

"That sort of transpersonal experience doesn't usually last too long. Mine was gut-wrenching while it did, I can tell you."

"I know."

"You *know*? You've had such an experience? Recently?"

"I've discovered quite a bit about the Reichart mother and son."

"The child prodigy?"

"Yes. And just tonight I read the account of the boy's death. He died tragically in a fire."

"Without fulfilling his incredible musical promise, of course."

"Yes."

"Did the mother witness the death?"

"Yes. After reading the article, I fell asleep in a chair, something I never do. I dreamt about the fire first in the mother's viewpoint, then in the child's. I felt the mother's horror and helplessness, as well as the boy's fear and physical pain. These feelings stayed with me long after I awoke. They are with me now, the feelings, I mean."

Meg waited for Krista to respond. The pause was a long one.

"Krista, are you there?"

"Yes, yes, I am. I'm sorry. Your story just turned my arms into gooseflesh. I don't like it, Meg."

"Why?"

"Well, for one thing, you say you never nap in a chair."

"So you're thinking I was kind of . . . used?"

"I don't know. I just don't."

"I told you about the smells that accompanied the two—dead flowers with the mother and burnt ash with the son. Tonight, both smells were here after the dream. That's why I needed to talk to you about the dual unity concept." Meg drew in a breath. "So you think it's possible?"

"Are you there alone, Meg?"

"Yes."

"Your husband?"

"Oh, he had his own experience and decided to head for the city."

"Marriage problems?"

Meg paused before responding. "Not unfixable."

"Meg, perhaps the conservative thing for you to do would be to join him."

"I expect that might happen next week."

"No, I mean tonight."

"Why?"

"We're sailing in uncharted waters for the most part. I've told you that before. Your openness may have tapped you into the tragedy of these two lives. Or perhaps these two . . . "

"Ghosts? You were going to say *ghosts* rather than *spirits*."

"I was."

"Because ghosts don't know that they're dead— "

"And they operate on negativity. They aren't angels, Meg. You've done your homework, and what you've found is that there was enough negativity in the circumstances of their deaths to power a small city. Chances are they want something."

"What?"

"I haven't a clue."

"But you think I might be in danger?"

A long pause, then, "Yes."

Meg took a deep breath. "There are still things I want to know. And I have an idea where to look."

"What? Where?"

"The what I don't know. Maybe it's just a matter of learning how I can reassure these—ghosts—in order to put their souls to rest."

"You're out of your depth here, Meg. What makes you think you can do that?"

"I don't know."

"And the where?"

"In the coach house. It stands on the same foundation as the barn in which the boy burned to death. I've had an aversion to the place since we moved here. But now I want to go in. I have to, for some reason."

"Listen to me, Meg, it's not a good idea."

"But it springs from my impulse voice, Krista, the one you told me about."

"You may only think that. It may spring from . . . their . . . influence. Wait until your husband is there with you."

"That may be a long time. Oh, don't worry, Krista. My friend Wenonah is coming to spend the night. I won't be alone."

"Good. That's something at least."

"Yes, well, thanks, Krista. You *have* helped."

"I'm glad. But remember my caution. I'm serious!"

"I understand."

"I hope to see you soon. It doesn't have to be in a professional environment, either."

"I'd like that. Bye, Krista, and thanks again."

"Goodbye."

Meg looked at her watch. It was 10:45 p.m. Wenonah wouldn't arrive for a good hour. Meg went into the bedroom for a sweater. The walk from the house to the coach house was a short one, but she vividly recalled the chill that had gone through her the last time she was in that building.

———— ∘◦◖∞◗◦∘ ————

Doctor Krista Peterhof allowed ten minutes, twenty, then a half-hour, to go by. The sick sensation in her stomach would not let up.

Meg's situation was more than disconcerting. Krista's mind kept picturing Meg as a splashing swimmer treading water— comfortable on the sun-drenched surface—and oblivious that the water activity had attracted dark, shadowy things below. Menacing things for which she was no match.

Krista's own impulse voice got the best of her. She went to the phone book.

She had been rude in their last conversation, she knew. Still, she had to voice a warning to someone.

It took only a minute to find the listing for K. Rockwell on Pine Grove Avenue.

Krista drew in breath and dialed.

"Hello?" The voice at the other end was sleepy and unfriendly.

TWENTY—THREE

We are not just highly evolved animals with biological
computers embedded inside our skulls; we are also
fields of consciousness without limits, transcending
time, space, matter, and linear causality.

Stanislav Grof

MEG UNLOCKED THE SIDE DOOR that led to the verandah
and stepped out. The balcony above protected her from the
light, misty rain. It was dark. The full moon was a prisoner of the
clouds and haze.

The columned porch had no steps or other point of entry, so
if she were to go out to the coach house she would have to retrace
her steps and exit the side door at the rear of the house. *If* she
were to— "

Meg realized now that she was giving herself an out, a chance
to reconsider her decision.

She stood at the north end of the verandah, facing the darkened
coach house, one hand upon the balustrade, the other holding
closed the sweater. Did she dare go in? What would she find?

As she stood there, her gaze fastened on the dilapidated coach
house, bits of the most recent dream flashed in her mind like a
strobe light. In the lighted moments she saw not the coach house,

but the original barn; not the two pairs of upstairs windows, but a single aperture. The building was ablaze. Meg felt as if she had one foot in the present and one foot in 1911.

Immediately, instinctively, she knew she was standing on the very spot on which Alicia Reichart had stood, helplessly watching the fire and smoke overcome her son.

Meg shuddered. How terrible it was, she thought—no, she seemed somehow to *know*, the empathy was so great—to watch one's own child die in so horrible a way. Her hand moved to her belly.

The moment passed. The experience seemed to heighten Meg's desire to go into the coach house. She turned around now and passed through the door leading into the dining room.

The key to the coach house padlock was on a huge ring of keys she and Kurt had been given upon the closing. She thought she had remembered Kurt's saying that he had put them in her grandmother's buffet. She looked through the antique that had fitted so snugly into the alcove, absently thinking what a shame it would be to have to move it out.

The ring was not in either of the two top drawers. Neither was it in the pair of cabinets beneath, nor in the wide, heavy drawer at the bottom. But as she stood up, she saw the ring sitting atop the buffet, big as life. She knew it had not been there a minute before. Or had it?

Meg picked up the ring and moved quickly to the rear now and stepped out of the side door into the drizzle and dark. Still no moon. The resounding effect of the ring of keys as she walked reminded her of a tintinnabulation of a tambourine.

It took only a minute or two to arrive at the overhang of the coach house door. The entrance was situated in the front, facing the drive, and to the left of the dilapidated, inoperable, double garage doors.

She fumbled through the keys, searching for the likely one for an old and rusty padlock. Several looked promising but didn't fit.

The dampness seemed to penetrate her skin. Her heart was racing. Why did she feel such urgency? Why did she feel like an interloper on her own property?

The fifth key turned.

The lock clicked, opened.

Meg removed the padlock, pulled open the door, and placed the lock—key and ring still attached—inside on the second stair.

She closed the door behind her.

She paused, peering up at what she knew was a long, straight, steep staircase. It was fully dark at the top, eerily silent.

Damn! She had not thought to bring a flashlight. Too bad, she wasn't about to go back for one.

Meg remembered now that they were paying a tiny separate electric bill for the place, and her hand reached for a nearby wall switch. It was round and mounted on the surface of the wall. It was old and loose to the touch. Meg flipped up the switch.

The bulb in a pot metal fixture at the top of the stairs flashed on, illuminating the dirty and well-worn stairs. Almost at once, the bulb sounded an alarming buzz, flickered momentarily, and went out, plunging the stairwell once again into darkness.

Meg had the presence of mind to turn the switch off. No sense in having the thing short out any more than it had. It could be dangerous. Going back for the flashlight was still a possibility, but she didn't want to afford herself the very real temptation of a full retreat.

Taking hold of the wooden banister to the right, she pulled herself slowly up the stairs.

At the top and to the left, a window provided a view of the backyard. She peered down into the gray and black mist, barely discerning white stepping stones leading to the alley. She felt her vertigo pull at her and looked away.

A closet was positioned at the top, its door now open. It appeared empty, but she dared not step into its void.

She moved to the right, in the direction of the apartment's four rooms. The bathroom—on her left—came first. She craned her neck, taking in the white of the walls and old porcelain fixtures that shone fuzzily through the gloom. Much of the plaster lay in heaps on the floor, victimized by frozen pipes of past years.

Another few steps brought her down the hall to the bedroom— on the right. From the hall she could see that it was small and empty. She could make out a few hangers and cellophane garment bags that littered the floor near the closet.

Meg continued on. The dining room was next. She turned left and entered it. A brass or pewter chandelier glinted darkly. She dared not touch the wall switch.

She passed quickly through the room to where she knew a tiny galley kitchen was situated. She was at the rear of the structure now where a small window looked down into the alley. She peered out. Nothing below was visible.

Even in the darkness, everything in the coach house seemed as it was when Mrs. Shaw had taken them through it. Nothing unusual, nothing out of place.

Meg chuckled to herself. Fine detective she was. She had thought that because little Claude had died on these premises she would find here the source of energy that had been disturbing their lives. It was not to be. The energy must be in the main house.

So much for my impulse voice!

It was then that she smelled it. Dead flowers—decaying violets—sickeningly sweet and rotten. Strong enough to gag her. It came on a cold breeze as if someone had passed nearby.

Meg felt blood rushing to her face, felt it pulsing at her temples. An icy hand seemed to grasp at her heart—the whole room grew suddenly cold. She could see her breath.

Meg wanted to run in the direction she had come, but her feet wouldn't move.

She listened.

There was only one room left to investigate—the living room.

Amazed—and appalled—she found herself moving in that direction. As if she had no will of her own.

She was in the hallway before she knew it. A right turn would provide an escape route. Her mind said *right*, but her feet moved left. Like in her dreams, she was not in control. Just a few steps would bring her into the living room.

She moved as if in slow motion. The small bit of living room in her sight line revealed nothing. But a faint glow seemed to emanate from the room's interior.

The other smell assaulted her now. The smell of ash, human ash.

Again, she thought of retreat. She wanted to run. But again her feet carried her forward—and all at once she was standing in the living room, her heart pumping like a puppy's, her face drained of blood.

There in front of the nonfunctional arts and crafts fireplace stood two figures, staring at Meg as if they had been waiting a very long time for her to come calling, yet certain that she would come to them.

Meg's first thought was that these were two real persons. How had two people come to be standing in this abandoned and locked building? She couldn't imagine. They were that real.

These were not spirits. Nothing filmy or fuzzy about them. Were they ghosts? No author of ghost stories had ever offered up figures like these. Not Henry James. Not Stephen King. They defied the stereotype. Meg was certain that if she conjured up the nerve to go over and touch them, she would find them made of matter.

Yet they seemed so still. Like statues and expressionless. She looked for the lift of the chests, the flare of nostrils, for surely they must be breathing. But there was no lift, no flare, no sound of breath in the room that—aside from the thump of her heart—was silent as a crypt.

It wasn't air that was key to their existence, she finally realized.

And perhaps this was their crypt. These were not living people. She shivered at the cold that had enveloped her, the fear that suffused her.

When had the boy's expression changed? He was smiling now. Or had he been smiling when she entered? She wasn't certain. The smile was simple and genuine, yet immeasurably sad. Take away the sadness and he was the image of the picture she had found in the Calumet Room. And he was the boy who had chased Rex up the stairs and out onto the balcony. He was Claude Reichart.

Yes, he seemed three-dimensional, flesh and blood, but as Meg studied him, she became aware of a facet that defied sense. A subtle luminescence pulsed and glowed about him, a kind of electricity that perhaps was his life—at least in the manner it was being manifested to her.

His smile was reaching out, warming Meg, taking her in like a harbor welcomes a ship long at sea. Her eyes became helplessly transfixed by his gaze. His were the eyes of emeralds.

Suddenly, she felt a rush of energy, an electrical charge within herself—starting in her feet—moving through her legs—streaming hotly upward through her body. This supersensible energy tore through her like a cyclone until she felt herself being carried with it—out of and away from her own body—and then toward and into the boy.

Meg had never taken any kind of hallucinatory drug, yet she was able to think to herself now—as this was happening—that this is what the experience of LSD must be like.

She felt at one with herself, with the boy, with the universe.

She was not merely feeling empathy for the boy. She was a part of him. His sense of sadness was all-pervasive, and it entered every area of her consciousness. She felt his tragedy, the tragedy of a life cut short in its prime, the tragedy of a talent never to be realized.

Then she was falling, spiraling deeper into what must be the core of the boy. The experience reminded her of the Flying Turns, a God-forsaken amusement ride that had made her very ill as a child.

There was no vertigo now, strangely, as she plunged into the space the boy inhabited. Darkness narrowed all about her as if she were enclosed in a sarcophagus. Then colored lights streamed past her at an astonishing speed—but it was she moving, not the lights. She knew that she had moved out of the boy's core, into a greater, wider expanse.

But the sadness that had been the boy's did not diminish. Conversely, it increased here, magnified many more times than the boy's. She came to feel—and she knew this instinctively—the sadness of every person who had died young, everyone who had died with his songs unsung, lives unlived.

The thought that this could only reflect the holotropic universe that Krista Peterhof had described, as well as Jung's positing of a collective unconscious, entered her own consciousness in a nanosecond.

Meg had never felt such sadness, such despair. She endured it for what seemed an eternity. When she felt she could take it no longer, that very thought seemed to empower her, and she realized she held the secret of withdrawal. Her mind called forth the energy, and it streamed—through her feet and legs—through her body—propelling her consciousness past prisms of light—through the tunnel of darkness—into and out of the boy's luminescent pulse—and into her own physicality.

She looked at little Claude. No speech was needed between them. Instead, an electrical current—a mental telepathy—left nothing unsaid, nothing misunderstood.

She understood his pain, suffered with him, consoled him. He knew that she comprehended his sadness. His smile, not without sadness, had widened slightly, again the change happening without her seeing it. Such was movement in their world.

An innate sense of accomplishment, of inner peace, descended on Meg like a golden nimbus. She became flushed with pride that she had been able to abate the child's pain. She had communicated to him that he was to let go of the past and give himself over to what was to come.

This is what has driven me here—to this house, to these souls. Meg believed that the validation of their pain would make it possible for them to make the full crossing to the other side, to lift them to what Krista had called the higher level of the astral sphere. No more clinging to a tragic past—or the physical world.

Meg became aware that the woman was standing closer to the boy now. Again, she had seen no movement. It was Claude's mother, of course—Alicia Reichart. She was dressed in black except for a bit of white luminescence at the wrists and neck. Her face was ageless—not as young as in the 1910 photograph, nor as old as she must have looked at the time of her suicide at fifty-four. The features were strong and attractive in the way some people call "handsome." And, yes, there was that mole on her left cheek.

Meg assimilated all of this information about the woman in an instant, for it only took that instant for her to realize that she should turn away.

But she could not.

The woman had already commanded a power that entranced Meg. The woman's eyes appeared colorless little pits that opened to—what? Grief? Yes—and more. This was not the sadness of a little boy. This was deep grief, deep regret, deeper anger.

Dangerous anger.

When the uninvited surge came from deep within Meg, attempting to propel her spirit from her and into Alicia—as had happened with Claude—her reaction to stop the energy flow was immediate—and just as powerless. She was dealing with a force beyond her own league. A lethal force.

She felt herself speeding toward the woman.

Just as the siren Circe drew in Odysseus, the woman pulled Meg to the vortex of her energy. She plummeted into a quarry of sorrow. This time the vertigo was present. As she fell—her stomach in turmoil—she experienced what she interpreted as the loss of a child. Iron gray grief pressed in on her, crushed her, raped her.

She had become one with Alicia Reichart.

As with Claude, however, the journey did not stop there. She passed into a dark tunnel, spiraling down into a wider, boundless world, the world of the collective unconscious. The grief— seemingly already limitless—became more acute as she found herself taking on—actually experiencing—the grief of every mother who had lost a child.

Time here lengthened, became a torture as the wailing women seemed to reach for her. Every moment brought with it new pain and hurt. She had been warned about being drawn into the lower astral realm. She sensed myriad beings flocking to her, draining energy from her, attempting to grasp hold of her, to drag her into their midst. Alicia and the others meant to keep her here. Nothing reigned here but evil.

Meg consciously worked to summon energy to counter whatever it was that caused her to enter this dimension. She prayed like never before, focusing, calling on light and life and all things good—and on God. She began to move upward—slowly at first—then faster, away from the reaching hands—through the great abyss—through the tunnel—and into the confines of Alicia Reichart's force.

It was here that she felt as if she were moving through an erupting volcano, one that flowed hot and red with pain and angst and anger.

At last, Meg found herself within her own form. She was staring at the woman. She knew now, instinctively, what the game was all about. It was all too clear that no reassurance or validation would hold back the flow of negativity within and from the woman. This was a lost soul. Meg had somehow been one with her, feeling the loss of her family, living her last years in an asylum, hanging herself in a cell—and most of all, never forgetting, never forgiving the loss of little Claude, the killing of his talent and future.

And yet, Meg made the attempt at consolation. She tried to communicate her feelings, her understanding, to the woman.

In a crosscurrent, the woman made known her desires to Meg. She wanted more than validation—she wanted Meg's full empathy and had for weeks been working to that end. She expected Meg to surrender her individuality, her soul, to her. And the soul of Meg's fetus would be surrendered to the energy that was Claude.

Meg swallowed hard and fear ran through her like a river. The woman plotted a kind of possession, and Meg's own holotropic experience told her that such a thing might actually be possible. It seemed a new twist on what Krista had labeled dual unity.

Panic boiled up within Meg. She could only blame herself. She had actually considered this possession scenario previously—and had scoffed at it. And before that, she had deliberately opened herself up to the forces in the house.

She had been a fool and now stood fully vulnerable before something evil and powerful. And what's more, she had endangered the life and soul of her unborn child.

Why hadn't she listened to Krista?

All right, I thought myself strong enough to deal with this. Now I will have to prove it.

Meg's body stiffened as she summoned a reserve she didn't know she had, wordlessly communicating to the woman now that she would be no party to her scheme. That she would resist. The woman was dead. Her time—and Claude's—had come and gone. It was terribly sad and tragic—but it was so. She must allow herself and her son to pass over, to experience whatever was next.

The energy that was Claude seemed receptive. Meg sensed that it had been his mother whose own intense goals and regrets held him to the lower realm of the astral plane.

The woman, however, was in no way receptive—and when Meg attempted to underscore her argument, Alicia Reichart let the stakes of the game be known—if Meg didn't submit to her will, neither she nor her child would live.

Meg's stomach dropped. She knew now there was no arguing

with, no convincing this woman who had died in an asylum, this woman who had waited decades for someone like Meg—and her child—to happen along. There was no saving Alicia Reichart. Meg could save only herself.

"Angels, and ministers of grace, defend us!" she cried.

She heeled about and ran. She felt the heat of anger, the stench of death, at her back, and under her feet the very floorboards vibrated.

The top of the stairs was dark as pitch. Meg stopped, afraid to go down, afraid to fall. She couldn't see the drop beneath her, but just knowing it was there brought on the old vertigo. She pressed her hands to her belly, her child.

"Angels, and ministers of grace, defend us!" Meg cried, knowing these were not her words, only that some recall of hers had brought them up. "Angels, and ministers of grace, defend us!"

Alicia had moved from the living room, had followed her. Meg could not detect her in motion, however. But with every blink of the eye, the woman appeared closer.

In this instant, Meg realized what the phenomenon reminded her of—a hologram! To watch the woman bearing down on her in this frenetic sort of motion was like looking into a hologram.

Somehow, the ghost of Alicia Reichart seemed all the more dangerous.

Meg's hand instinctively went for the wall, found its mark, pushed the switch up.

The light above her came on with an explosion. Flames shot out from the hanging fixture and moved in two directions—along the ceiling down into the stairwell—as well as down the hall and toward the figure of the woman.

Meg started down the stairs, holding onto the banister, running, each stair bringing a jolt, knowing even in her panic what a fall could mean for the baby.

At the bottom, she found the door closed tight and fast. As if it had been locked! She looked at the step where she had left the padlock. It was gone. She knew this was the work of Alicia.

Meg looked up the stairway and could see nothing but flames. No escape there.

At that moment, at the top of the stairs, she witnessed a great flare and an explosion that she could only think was the energy that had been Alicia Reichart.

Meg had no time to feel relief. She had to escape—or face her own death. The hall was filling with smoke, and she began to cough.

She saw that there was a door that led into the garage. She turned the knob and the door opened.

Meg stepped down. It was dark inside. She stumbled about in the direction of the front garage doors, metal doors she knew to be broken in their closed position. Kurt had tried unsuccessfully to open them the first weekend. But they were her only chance.

She could smell the smoke seeping down through the floorboards and air ducts. The building would burn to its foundation, just as the old barn had done.

She felt one of the rusty doors and tried it. It wouldn't budge. Hunching over, she tried to move it with the strength of her shoulders and hips. Its locking apparatus was rusted solidly in place. If Kurt had been unable to open them, what hope did she have?

The smoke was thickening now. She could hear the voracious roar of the fire above her. The materials of the coach house were like tinder that had dried for ninety years. Pockets of the fire were beginning to break through the floor and lick at the underside of the floorboards. How could fire move so rapidly?

Meg knew to get down on the cement floor for the best air. She did so and crawled to the other door. Its lock moved! *Thank God!*

Yet the door did not lift.

She was starting to choke now.

She prayed to hear sirens soon, prayed that some neighbor had seen the flames.

From her lying position, she pushed at the door.

It held firm.

When she took her hands away, she felt warm liquid running down her right hand. She was bleeding, cut on metal that had partially rusted away.

Ignoring the cut, she thought that enough of the weakened door might give way, allowing for an escape. Meg maneuvered her body so that her feet pressed against the door's bottom. She kicked out. Again and yet again.

So rusted was the door that metal fragments began to fall away.

Lying on her back, through the smoke she could see the flames fully digesting the floorboards above her and spreading to the joists. The heat would soon be as deadly as the smoke.

How long until the boards and timbers started falling in on her—trapping her—killing her as surely as little Claude had been burned to death on this spot?

She could see now that the hole in the bottom of the door was big enough to get her head out—but would her shoulders fit?

She had no choice but to try. There was no more time to turn her body around and kick again. This was her only chance.

Lying on her back, Meg pushed her head through, taking in the clear night air, and tried to squeeze through the lacework of broken and rusty metal, ragged metal she felt cutting into her shoulders and upper arms. She thought she heard sirens.

With a great effort, she pushed her shoulders through, the metal ripping through her blouse, tearing at her skin. Slowly, slowly, she moved with caterpillar-like movements out of the burning building.

As she felt herself losing consciousness, someone gripped her arms now and dragged her away from the building.

Her first thought was that it was Kurt.

"Meg, hold on, for God's sake! The ambulance is here."

Before descending into a welcome oblivion, Meg realized the voice was not Kurt's.

It was Wenonah's.

TWENTY—FOUR

MEG KNEW THAT SHE WAS in a hospital bed before she opened her eyes. She had worked in a hospital too long not to recognize the smells and sounds—even in the middle of the night. Not to mention the hardness of the mattress and coarseness of the linens.

She sensed, too, someone sitting vigil nearby. She could hear the almost imperceptible breathing rhythm. She knew who it was. She pretended to sleep, putting off the strain of communication for the time being, preferring to let her mind drift, then find focus in good time.

Was the boy all right? She sensed nothing wrong there, and he moved in her womb—she thought—as if to reassure her.

Meg felt quietly victorious. She had met her nemesis—the ghost that stood between her and happiness in the house—and she had triumphed. Only now did she realize what a terrible gamble it had been. She had positioned herself against the unknown and non-physical world and into the bargain she had put her unborn at risk. Knowing what she knew now, she would never attempt it again.

Alicia Reichart had suffered a horrific tragedy in the death of her little Claude. And she wasted years of her life in mourning and regrets—and the negativity did not end with death. She somehow held on to her son's soul, too, holding him back from ascending to the next astral realm, keeping him tied to her own hell.

Nonetheless, Meg realized that she still held a great empathy for the woman. It had become a part of her. She would not try to rid herself of it. She would instead store it away deep within her—and come to forget it. She prayed that little Claude had moved on—but she doubted she would ever know for certain.

Meg's body was bruised and torn, yet she felt a kind of serene happiness that stemmed from something more than victory over Alicia. She had taken away from her experience with the woman two things: the awareness of time and energy lost on things irretrievable and the ability to reevaluate her own life.

For twenty years she had been full of regret for a love that had not been meant to be. All that was over now. Forever. Later, she would think the drugs she had been given fired her imagination, for she thought of her love for Pete passing from her now, becoming a kind of balloon of pale pink, imagined severing a string that anchored it to the ground, imagined releasing it into the air.

Not with regrets. With relief. With a blessed happiness.

As the balloon ascended, receding from sight, becoming smaller and smaller, disappearing, Meg became ebullient. She felt free—was free—for the first time in twenty years.

She had let go.

She could feel the warm tears streaming down her face. She thought back to her meeting with Dr. Peterhof—Krista—and the holographic theory. Meg felt more content than she ever had. She was but an image in a hologram, but her future felt as boundless as the universe that held that image.

Meg felt her tears being brushed away. She opened her eyes.

She found herself staring into two blue pools.

"What is it, Meg?" Kurt asked. "Are you all right?"

She smiled. "Yes."

He squeezed her hand. "Forgive me for leaving you behind. I

was stupid. I never understood your attachment to the house—how strong it is."

"And you do now?"

He shrugged. "The how maybe—but not the why."

"I was pretty stubborn. What did you call it—my 'whim of iron'?"

"I'm getting used to that stubborn streak."

"The house is at peace, Kurt. I know it. The spirits—ghosts, rather—have moved on. The negativity is gone."

"You're sure?"

"Yes."

"Well, so is the coach house. To the ground. All we have to do is raze the foundation."

"I won't make you stay, Kurt. We can move if that's what you want."

"Actually, I was hatching a plot to buy a three-bedroom across the street from the condo—in Wenonah's building, The Pattington. I know how much you admire it." His eyes narrowed, assessing her reaction. "Would you like that?"

Meg smiled tentatively.

Kurt understood. "More than living in my condo—but less than living on Springfield Street?" His eyes narrowed. "Am I right?"

Meg was silent for a minute, then said, "Life is compromise. I won't make you live there."

"Meg, if I'm with you, I'm happy. Maybe I can get a job out here. —There's just one thing."

"What's that?"

"For the first year—no, let's say for the duration, *you* run the washer and dryer."

TWENTY—FIVE

WENONAH HAD NOT BEEN OUT to the house since that night. Not that she hadn't offered to come out, but she sensed Meg and Kurt were operating on a new level. They were having, it seemed, a kind of second honeymoon. The baby's birth, however, called for an appearance.

She pulled into the drive now. The coach house was gone, foundation and all. She was glad for that.

The house had been newly painted. A white that glowed luminously in the sunshine. It couldn't have looked any better in 1910, she thought.

Kurt met her at the door. Meg was in the dining room putting the finishing touches on the lunch. She was slim again, slimmer than she, damn it, and radiant.

Of course, Wenonah knew what motherhood could do—not from experience, not yet. But body clock or no, she had not given up on the other half of the human race.

Meg hugged her with all the old enthusiasm. The baby, a pink bundle with fine, flaxen hair and emerald eyes, was beautiful. He had a marvelous temperament, Meg told her. Indeed, as they ate lunch, he sang to them from the bassinet nearby.

Kurt was happy, too, she could tell. Of course, he might be happier—and she'd like him a lot more—if his job didn't support the new for-profit status of the hospital which entailed the elimination of dedicated health workers and the decline of patient care. And it was hard to forgive his leaving Meg alone that night.

Watching them, however, made Wenonah vow to herself not to be so judgmental.

She smiled now at something Kurt was saying about the child, thinking that one day he might see the light and that as long as he was good to—and for—Meg, she'd make the attempt to accept him.

Not long after lunch, Wenonah made a move to go. The preparations for the meal and preoccupation with the baby had tired Meg.

"I love ya, girl," Wenonah said, as she embraced Meg.

Meg and Kurt insisted she hold the baby for a few minutes, and doing so gave her more pleasure than she would have imagined. As she held him, she thought how such a little package was able to change the configuration of adult lives.

After a while she gave the baby over to Meg to nurse.

Motherhood had changed Meg, Wenonah thought as she moved toward the door. She hoped to stay friends with Meg—but she doubted that she'd ever be *needed* again. Passages in life were like this.

There was something else about Meg, too, a deeper change that was unnamable and almost imperceptible. What was it?

"Thanks for coming, Win," Kurt said on the porch. "Meg really enjoyed having you here."

"He's a beautiful child. You've got two to look after now, Kurt." It was a passive-aggressive barb, and Wenonah cursed herself before it was fully out of her mouth. She was reminding him of past failures. She felt a twinge of shame—so much for killing off judgmental attitudes.

"I know," he said, evidently accepting her comment at face value.

A large, unmarked truck was pulling up in front of the house.

"Expecting something?" Wenonah asked.

Kurt laughed. "We got what we expected, Win."

Wenonah laughed, too.

The driver jumped from the truck's cab.

"Probably wants directions," Kurt said.

As the stout driver came up the walk, a second delivery man jumped to the ground and moved toward the rear of the truck.

"Help you?" Kurt asked.

"I need a signature from . . . " Coming to the porch steps, the man glanced down at the form on his clipboard, then finished with, "Meg Rockwell."

"She's busy right now. I'll sign. I'm her husband."

When the man reached the top step, Kurt scribbled his name, his eyes searching the invoice.

The man returned a copy to Kurt and retreated.

Kurt studied it again.

"What is it?" Wenonah asked.

Kurt shrugged. "I'll be damned if I know. All I see are model numbers." He called now to the driver, who was boarding the lift at the rear of the truck. "Hey, what is it we're getting?"

"Oh, I figured you knew, buddy," he called back. "It's a piano."

Wenonah felt something foreign ignite and stir within herself now. "Sweet Jesus," she said under her breath. Her heart raced. She turned to Kurt.

His face was a mask. Inscrutable. Had he paled, just a little? Had the lines about his mouth curved a bit to reflect his reaction?

And his eyes—those cool, blue fathomless eyes—they told her nothing.

THE POLAND TRILOGY

BY JAMES CONROYD MARTIN

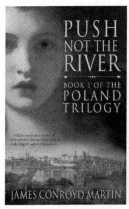 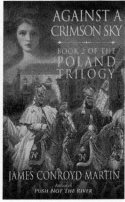 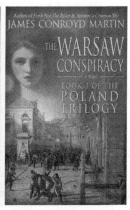

BASED ON THE DIARY OF a Polish countess who lived through the rise and fall of the Third of May Constitution years, 1791-94, *Push Not the River* paints a vivid picture of a tumultuous and unforgettable metamorphosis of a nation—and of Anna, a proud and resilient woman. *Against a Crimson Sky* continues Anna's saga as Napoléon comes calling, implying independence would follow if only Polish lancers would accompany him on his fateful 1812 march into Russia. Anna's family fights valiantly to hold onto a tenuous happiness, their country, and their very lives. Set against the November Rising (1830-31), *The Warsaw Conspiracy* depicts partitioned Poland's daring challenge to the Russian Empire. Brilliantly illustrating the psyche of a people determined to reclaim independence in the face of monumental odds, the story features Anna's sons and their fates in love and war.

NEXT FROM JAMES CONROYD MARTIN

THE BOY WHO WANTED WINGS

The Story of the First 9-11
Release date: 2015

IN JULY OF 1683 VIENNA came under siege by the full brunt of the Ottoman Empire so that by 11 September it stood as the main outpost of Christian Europe. The citizens were starving and the walls of the city were giving way. Vienna was about to fall under the guns and mines of the Ottomans. Its collapse would mean plundered European cities, Christian slaves, and forced conversions. Allied European armies under the supreme command of Polish King Jan III Sobieski arrived not an hour too soon. The King descended the hill, riding at the van of his legendary winged hussars—armed with lances, pistols, and sabres—and an army of 40,000 against 140,000. Reputedly, the sight and sound of the wings of feathers attached to the hussars frightened both man and beast. Panic swept through the enemy and the battle was over within three hours. Europe had been saved from the enemy.

The Boy Who Wanted Wings is the story of a young Tatar boy adopted into a Polish peasant household. Aleksy has a long-held dream of becoming a Polish Hussar, a dream complicated by a forbidden love for a nobleman's daughter. It is only when the Ottomans seek to conquer Europe, coming at Vienna in 1683 for a monumental and decisive battle, that fate intervenes, providing Aleksy with opportunities—and obstacles.

AN EXCERPT

DESPITE SOMETIMES BEING LABELED *THE Tatar* by some of his peers, as well as by some adults who snarled at him, Aleksy had been content to stay within the cocoon of Polishness he had come to know. Even though as the years went by and he became less fearful of venturing away from the family that had taken him in, he was afraid that doing so would hurt them. And so he had embraced Christianity and the Polish way of living.

But then there were times like these when he felt removed from everything and everyone around him. Oh, he knew that the boundaries of class set a count's daughter upon a dais and well out of his reach, but to think now that the fortune of his birth and an appearance that reflected a coloring and visage that reached back to parents and ancestors made the chasm between him and the girl in yellow so much deeper and—despite logic—somehow a fault of his own.

Still, he thought, his acceptance of things Polish could be providential—should he ever have the opportunity—slight as it was—of meeting the girl in yellow.

About halfway up the mountain, he came to a little clearing that jutted out over a cleared field. He dismounted. His eyes fastened on the activity below. This is what he had come for, and so he put the count's daughter from his mind. Brooding on what cannot be, he determined, would come to nothing.

The company of hussars on the field seemed larger today, at least fifty, Aleksy guessed. They were being mustered into formation now, their lances glinting in the sun, the black and gold pennants flying. There would be none of the usual games, it seemed, no jousting, no running at a ring whereby the lancers would attempt to wield their lance so precisely as to catch a small ring that hung from a portable wooden framework. Today they were forming up for sober and orderly maneuvers. He wondered at their formality.

Aleksy took note of the multitude of colors below and the little mystery resolved itself. Whereas on other occasions the men, some very young and generally of modest noble birth and means, wore outer garments of a blue, often cheap material, today they had been joined by wealthier nobles who could afford wardrobes rich in the assortment of color and material. These men—in their silks and brocades and in their wolf and leopard skins or striped capes— gathered to the side of the formation to watch and deliver commentary. Some of these were the Old Guard of the Kwarciani, the most elite of Hussars permanently stationed at borderlands east of Halicz to counter raids by Cossacks and Tatars unfriendly to the Commonwealth of Lithuania and Poland. Their reviews would be taken, no doubt, with great solemnity. Every soldier would make every effort to impress them. In recent years the group's numbers had been reduced by massacres and talk had it that they were eager to replenish their manpower. Perhaps a few of the novices below would be chosen to join the Kwarciani.

Some place at his core went cold with jealousy. If only he were allowed to train as a hussar. He could be as good as any of them. *Better.* No one he knew was more skillful at a bow than he. He could show those hussars a thing or two about the makings of an archer—even though he had come to realize fewer and fewer of the lancers bothered to carry a bow and quiver. The majority had come to disparage the art of archery in favor of pistols, relying instead on the lance, a pair of pistols, and a sabre.

Naturally enough, there was no disdain for the lance, the very lifeblood and signature weapon of the hussar army. Aleksy smiled to himself when he thought of his own handcrafted lance. Through his father he had made friends with Count Halicki's old stablemaster, Pawel, who one magical day had allowed him to peruse an old lance once used by the count. Having fashioned his own bow and arrows, Aleksy was already an expert in woodcraft when he took the measurements of the lance and carefully replicated it, creating it from a seventeen foot length of wood cut in halves and hollowed out as far as the rounded handguard at the lower end, thus reducing its weight. The shorter section managed by the lancer was left solid wood for leverage purposes. Finding glue that would bind the two halves together had been a challenge, but an off-hand comment by Borys about a Mongolian recipe using a tar made from birch bark brought success.

Aleksy's thoughts conjured an elation that was only momentary, for he thought now how he had had to hide away his secret project under a pile of hay in the barn—and unless he should happen to be practicing with it one day in the forest when a wayward boar might come his way, he would never be able to use it. The thought of mounting a plow horse like Kastor with it instead of riding atop one of the Polish Arabians strutting below made him burn with—what? Indignation? Embarrassment? Humiliation—yes, he decided, humiliation was the most accurate descriptor.

Inexplicably, the thought of the girl in yellow once again seized him, lifting him, causing his heart to catch. Would he exchange one dream for the other? Life as a hussar for life with her?

He thought he just might risk anything to succumb to her charms.

CONNECT WITH THE AUTHOR

WEBSITE/BLOG
http://www.JamesCMartin.com

FACEBOOK
https://www.facebook.com/pages/
James-Conroyd-Martin-Author/29546357206?ref=hl

TWITTER
@JConMartin

61268233R10136

Made in the USA
Lexington, KY
06 March 2017